REINDEER GAMES

N.R. WALKER

COPYRIGHT

BLURB

Reindeer Games Definition: activities to exclude outsiders

Industrial-art student Leif Caldwell and his best friend win tickets to the hottest party in town, the annual masquerade Christmas gala at the upmarket nightclub, Evoque. Not a gig they could ever afford to attend or buy costumes for, so Leif makes their masks. Given the holiday theme and the play on words, he makes a set of striking reindeer antlers and intends to have the night of his life.

Vintage Ridge's resident millionaire and owner of Evoque, Russ Quarrington, hates the holiday season because it reminds him of everything he's lost. All the money and success in the world can't fill the void in his heart, and this year he's particularly bereft. With the gala looming, his personal assistant insists Russ attends and that he wear a mask that offers anonymity, and hopefully find some festive cheer. Bored with the guys in town and tired of men only wanting him for his money, he reluctantly agrees.

But when Russ sees a mysterious man with a magnificent reindeer antlers and mask, he's instantly intrigued. Even when their masks are removed, Leif has no idea who Russ really is, and what Russ discovers is a man who understands him. And for the first time ever, a man who doesn't want what Russ has. This time, it's Russ who wants what Leif has, what money can't buy.

Russ and Leif are about to learn that sometimes *Reindeer Games* are the only games worth playing.

For the first 90 days of this title's publication, all sales and page reads will be donated to *Twenty10,* Sydney.

REINDEER GAMES is part of a multi-author series of books that take place in the same fictional town. Each story can be read in any order. The connecting element in the Ace's Wild series is an adult store owned by Ace and Wilder. The main characters from each book will make at least one visit to Ace's Wild, where they'll buy a toy to use in their story! The only characters who crossover to each book are Ace and Wilder. And with various heat levels, there's sure to be something for everyone!

REINDEER GAMES

N.R. WALKER

CHAPTER ONE

RUSS QUARRINGTON SAT in his office, gazing out over the view of the small city of Vintage Ridge, staring into that space between past and present, not really seeing anything at all. His mind had wandered. Again. His heart was heavy. He told himself it was the time of year—winter, Christmas —that affected him this way. Melancholy settled over him much like the blanket of cold that settled over the city outside his window.

He was thirty-four and had every physical thing in his life that he could ever need. He'd built a business and real-estate empire with a portfolio people only dreamed of. He had a fleet of great staff, had a mansion, cars, expensive suits, watches, a wine cellar, and a budding art collection.

Material things, he conceded. No emotional attachments, no personal relationships.

He was alone, and once upon a time, he'd thrived on that. He'd used it as the driving force to propel himself forward, to succeed. To be everything he was today. He'd refused any human interaction that might distract him from

1

his goals. *Succeed at all costs* had been his mantra for sixteen years.

But now the loneliness was a pool of inky-black water lapping at his feet. Well, it began at his feet. Now he waded waist-deep in it.

It's just the time of year, he told himself. *Christmas is never easy.*

He had no family, no close friends, no boyfriend, no lover. No one.

It was his choice. Well, the absence of family wasn't his choice. When given the ultimatum of being a part of his family or being gay, he chose the truth. His only truth. If he had chosen his family, it would have killed him anyway, to not be true, to not be his true self. So he chose honesty and integrity. He chose life.

He didn't regret it.

After sixteen years, he didn't miss them anymore.

Except at Christmastime.

Like now.

December and winter always hit him hard, right in the solar plexus, under his sternum, and inside his ribs. It felt like a lump of hot concrete. Heavy, and hard to ignore.

It was always worse this time of year, and each year it got a little harder than the year before.

There was a quick knock on the door before it opened, and Caleb walked in with his eyes glued to his iPad. Russ didn't need to check the time. Caleb said he'd be here at 2:00 p.m., so Russ knew it would be precisely 2:00 p.m. Everything about Caleb was precise. His appearance: impeccable suit, short and neatly styled hair, defined eyebrows, and square jaw. He was angular, sharp, and incredibly efficient. He'd been Russ's PA for five years and knew every facet, every detail, every schedule, every appointment.

He was also the closest thing Russ had to a best friend. Which Caleb would probably find horrifying and incredibly sad because Russ was sure Caleb wouldn't even think of him as any kind of friend, let alone a good friend. Least of all a best friend.

Christ. I need to make some changes in my life . . .

Caleb sat in the seat opposite Russ's desk and had still barely looked up from his iPad screen. "Okay, so we have a few things to go over before Friday. City planning meeting for the rezoning of Providence Street is tomorrow at ten, meeting with the bank and insurance broker tomorrow at two. I've sent both appointments to your calendar. We should close on the metro apartment if the real-estate attorney does his goddamned job, deeds and covenants pending, and the final preparations of the masquerade ball are all but done. I've requested the final marketing proofs by five o'clock today. Oh, and we still need to find a designer for the loft. I sent you a shortlist, just some recommendations . . ."

Russ heard everything Caleb had said but didn't exactly need to reply. In fact, Russ was seriously beginning to wonder if he needed to be here at all. Caleb had everything under control.

"Okay, what's wrong?" Caleb asked, clipped and to the point.

"Nothing's wrong," Russ replied, his voice hoarse from disuse. God, how long had it been since he'd spoken to someone? This morning's barista had spoken, and Russ was sure he'd replied out loud . . . He'd meant to. Christ. "Sorry. I've been distracted. There was nothing wrong with any of what you said. In fact, you're so good at what you do, I was just wondering if I needed to be here at all."

"That doesn't sound like nothing's wrong."

Russ looked back out over the city, shrouded in winter. "Maybe I need to go sit on a beach somewhere. Or buy a new car. Or a motorcycle."

"A motorcycle?" Caleb's eyes went comically wide. "Uh, I can think of things that are less likely to kill you . . ."

"What about a boat?"

"Yes, because crashing and drowning is better than crashing and skidding along gravel."

"Or maybe I should take a cooking class," Russ added, then shook his head at how ridiculous he sounded. "God, I hate cooking. Maybe I should volunteer somewhere. In a soup kitchen or for the Pride festival."

Caleb's sigh was long and knowing. "Those are some great ideas, Russ. But just answer me this. How long have I been telling you to take a vacation?"

"Years."

"And have you?"

"Well, I've been busy . . ."

"Which is why you need a vacation."

"I need to stay here," Russ countered, though it was hardly with an ounce of conviction. "My businesses—"

"Your businesses are prime examples of effective and efficient management." Caleb had his serious face on. "Your teams are well-structured, well-balanced, and well-versed in procedure and protocol. You could leave for a month and there wouldn't even be a blip on the radar."

Russ stared at him. Because feeling unnecessary and unwanted was just what he needed to add to his loneliness. "Gee, thanks."

"That's not what I meant," Caleb added apologetically.

"What I meant was, you're so good at what you do, your entire business model is perfect. You could have a month's vacation and the wheels will not fall off; every cog will turn, just as it should. You *should* have a month off."

A month? Russ almost broke out in hives at the thought. "A month?" He shook his head. "Yeah, not ever gonna happen."

"Take a week. Hell, take a weekend."

"I know, I try to, but then something comes up."

"Something that one of your teams can fix, or it can wait until you get back." Caleb raised an eyebrow, then looked at his iPad. "I can book you something right now. It'll be a complete surprise."

"No, please don't. I can't . . . I need more time . . . and I need to know where I'm going. I can't just do some mystery vacay thing." He shuddered at the thought.

Caleb stared at him for a long, uneasy moment. He tapped a finger on the side of his iPad, the way he did when he was thinking. "Okay, a compromise. You need a change of scenery, agreed?" Caleb asked, not giving Russ the time to reply. "The masquerade ball next weekend, you're going."

"Well, yes, of course I am. It's the Quarrington Annual Christmas Charity Gala at *my* nightclub. I have to go."

"No, you're *going*, going. Not as the owner or organizer or benefactor. As in, attending with a masquerade mask on, having a few drinks, maybe talk with a guy or two. Find some festive cheer."

"Festive what?"

"Exactly," Caleb said seriously. "That is exactly my point." Then his face and his tone softened. "I know this time of year isn't easy for you, but perhaps you should make new memories. I think volunteering your time at some local shelters throughout the year and not just at Christmas is also a great idea, and I'll see what I can find out for you on that front. But for now, let's agree that this year you'll at least try and have some fun."

"Caleb, I don't know . . ."

"It's the perfect opportunity," he countered quickly. "Complete anonymity with the mask. You can have some fun without the added pressure of anyone knowing it's you."

Russ opened his mouth to object.

"Great. It's settled," Caleb said, standing up. He was already tapping and scrolling on the screen of his iPad. "I'll organize your mask and whatever else you need. Leave the details up to me."

He started for the door. "Caleb, wait," Russ called out. Caleb stopped and turned, and Russ had every intention of telling him there was absolutely no way he was going to dress up for his Christmas gala night. But when he tried to form the words, when he tried to refuse, something stopped him. *Did he want to do this? Could he do this?* The truth was, he had nothing to lose. So instead of saying no, he sighed. "I want classy and sophisticated. You make me look like a candy cane or a Santa's Helper and you're fired. I mean it."

Caleb laughed. "No jolly Santa or naughty elf outfits. Got it. Oh," he added, his hand on the door. "One suggestion . . ."

Russ resisted rolling his eyes. "Yes?"

"You're familiar with Ace's Wild? It's a specialty—"

Russ put his hand up. "I know what it is. Or rather, who they are."

Caleb grinned. "I have it on good authority that's where a lot of the guys are getting props for the gala night. Maybe you could stop in and see them." He had a wicked gleam in his eye, almost a wink. "Tell Ace I said hi." And without another word, he disappeared and the door closed quietly behind him.

Great. Just fucking great. Russ spun to gaze out across the city again, this time wondering what the hell he'd just agreed to.

CHAPTER TWO

LEIF CALDWELL LOOKED around his workshop, searching for inspiration. He loved this space, and although he'd worked in shops that were bigger, newer, with every tool and prop he could ever need, there was nothing like being in the workshop at the back of his mother's house.

Fifty years ago it had been a garage. Timber construction, compact dirt floor, with shelves along the end wall, a worktop that ran down the right side. The hinges on the barn-style doors at the front protested with age and rust; the small window rattled with every breeze. The old shingled roof leaked every now and then, and when it was cold like this, the drafts that whistled through could almost freeze Leif to death.

But there was an earthiness to it, a combination of familiar scents that transported him back to his childhood, to his teenage years, and it fortified that creative side in him and reminded him of who he was. The smell of wood shavings, oil, leather, soldering rods, paint, and turpentine was his happy place.

Actually, the smell of his mom's fresh-baked banana

bread was his happy place. The smell of the workshop was home.

The workshop at college had never smelled like this, nor had any studio he'd worked out of. And no other workspace could spark inspiration like this one could. Leif could lose hours in here, designing, creating, feeling the grain of the wood or the rigidity of a length of cast iron. The stretch of leather or the softness of fabric and feathers.

He sat on the old barstool and looked around the workshop, running his hand over the smooth edge of the countertop. It was worn from years and use, Leif smiled as he put pieces together in his mind of what he would make. Taking his old notepad, he began to sketch . . .

His best friend Jamie had won tickets to the party of the year. Every holiday season there was a masquerade ball at Evoque, the hottest gay nightclub in town. It was some charity event the owner put on, and every year people vied for tickets. Every year, people dreamed of going. They only sold a set number of tickets, and it was that exclusivity that had the gay scene in town salivating.

And Jamie had won two tickets on Evoque's Instagram contest. Of course he was taking Leif. They'd been best friends forever, and they were both single at the same time, which didn't happen too often. Jamie's last boyfriend had been a bit of a dick, and Leif's last fling had lacked spark. So when he won the tickets, there wasn't anyone else Jamie said he'd rather go with him.

The only problem was, Evoque was upscale and expensive, and Leif and Jamie were . . . not. Leif had grown up in the part of town where money was scarce. His mom worked hard, had five foster kids—Leif included—and while they never had cool clothes with labels or cell phones like other kids in school, they always had food on the table, in a house full of love. Jamie lived three doors down, and he spent more time at Leif's place than his own. Leif's mom always welcomed him into her house and treated him like he was another one of hers, and she'd bake Jamie's favorite oat and maple syrup cookies on his birthday. It's just how it was in Leif's mom's house. It's how it still was today.

To save himself a few precious dollars, he was going to make his own masquerade mask.

He sketched a few design ideas, though usually his best work was done when he let his hands and mind make and create on the fly. Most often, his finished product barely resembled what he'd originally sketched.

So he began with the basics: the mold and fit of the mask, general shape, and medium. He began with simple black leather and shaped, trimmed, and primped it into the usual beginnings of a masquerade mask.

Boring, he thought, but it was a start. He added black press studs to the outer top of it, and he braided long black strands of leather to secure the mask. When tied off around the head, they would almost form a ponytail down his back.

"Hey," a familiar voice said from the door. Jamie slipped in and closed the door behind him, but not fast enough to stop the blast of cold air that rushed through. "Shit, it's cold out there."

"Oh, hey," Leif said with a smile.

Jamie was holding a coffee mug. "Your mom said you'd been out here for a few hours and thought you could use this."

"I take it you've already had a cup," Leif replied, taking the mug.

"Yep. And a grilled cheese. No one makes them like your mom."

Leif snorted at that. "I'm beginning to think you only put up with me for the food."

"Not at all," he said with a grin. "But seriously, it wouldn't hurt if you took some cooking lessons from her."

"Or you could." Leif sipped his coffee. "Ready for next weekend?"

"Nope. Thought we could go looking for ideas. There's a costume place across town. They might have something." Jamie shrugged. "Though I'll need your help because I'm clueless. What the hell do people wear to masquerade parties anyway? I keep picturing Zorro or a Ninja Turtle."

Leif laughed. "Mikey the Ninja Turtle isn't exactly sexy. Here, try this on." He took the mask he'd been playing with and held it up. "I was making this for me, but I'm not sure . . ."

Jamie's eyes went wide. "Holy shit. Is that a whip?"

"If you want it to be," Leif answered with a grin. "Versatile and functional is key for any great design."

Jamie laughed. "Hmm, versatile and fucktional. Two of my favorite words."

Leif fixed the mask to Jamie's face, adjusted it to his cheeks and forehead and tied the braids of leather at the back.

"Uh, Leif," he said. "It's a bit dark."

Leif chuckled. "Because I haven't punched out the eye holes yet."

Jamie shook his head a little. "I like the whip down my back, not gonna lie."

"You kinky fuck," Leif said with a smile. "I can add more. Make it a cat-o'-nine-tails." That gave him an idea. "I could add some cat ears if you want?"

Jamie's smile became a grin. "Hell yes. Because nothing says *pussy for rent* more than cat ears and a cat-o'-nine-tails."

Leif laughed and undid it. "I'll need to make a few adjustments, but it's yours."

"Man, that's so cool. Thank you." Then he stopped. "But what will you wear? I don't wanna take yours."

"Nah, it was just my first trial run. I was just going for ideas. And anyway, it's not really a me-mask."

"What are you gonna make for you?"

"Dunno yet. But I like the animal theme. I'll think of something."

"Boys?" Leif's mom called out. "Can I get your help for a sec?"

They opened the workshop doors and saw his mom wrestling with a set of gardening shears and the row of shrubs along the fence line. The best part of living on the outskirts was the house backing onto woods. Growing up, his brothers and sisters hated having to ride their bikes everywhere, but for Leif, having the trees and woods to escape to was perfect. He'd sketch, take leaves and twigs, and make art or furniture. Since he was a kid, he'd made his mom birthday gifts, and she still had them in the house. There was a lampshade of twigs and twine, picture frames, a napkin holder, and a wall clock. He'd bought an old clock from the thrift store for a few bucks and used the mechanism but made the clock himself from a fallen log. He'd sawed, sanded, and carved until he had it perfect, drilled a hole for the mechanism, and presto, he had a working clock. He'd been fifteen, and for ten years, that clock had sat above his mom's mantel.

"Here, Mom, let me get that," Leif said, relieving her of the shears. "What kind of prune are we doing? A trim or a full haircut?"

"A healthy trim, thanks, love," she said. She pruned this

time every year, but with two strong, young guys in her house, she shouldn't have to. She did enough for them.

Leif trimmed and Jamie grabbed the rake and cleaned up all the clippings, and in no time they had the line of shrubs and trees looking much neater. Jamie stacked the twigs and small branches near the woodpile. Once dried out, they'd make good kindling next year for the woodfire. Leif put the shears away and helped Jamie with the last of the cleaning up when he noticed Jamie had put a pile of twigs to the side.

"What are those for?"

"You," he replied. "I know you'd be rifling through 'em anyway. Thought I'd save you some time."

Leif smiled. Jamie knew him well, that was for certain.

"Not sure what they'd be good for," Jamie said, raking up some dead leaves. "Some unforeseen masterpiece, no doubt."

Leif picked up a twig. It was about a foot long with several offshoots, and he held it in his hands for a second, looking out into the woodlands.

"Whatever idea you're getting right now," Jamie said, "you're welcome."

Leif laughed and rummaged through the pile until he found another similar twig. Then he took a handful of the raked leaves. "I know what I'm doing for my mask."

Jamie looked at what Leif was holding, then shook his head with disbelief. "I will take your word for that, my friend."

"Come on," Leif said, opening the doors to the workshop again. "I'll do one more fit of your mask. Did you still want to go to the costume place?"

"No need now," Jamie replied. "But if I don't have to

pay for a costume mask, you have to let me buy you something."

"You don't have to pay for anything," Leif replied. "That's not why I made your mask."

"I know it's not. But I know exactly what we need, and they're having a holiday sale."

"Jamie," he tried.

"Shut up and let me do this. How often do we get to do this?" he asked, his eyes serious. "Never. And are we ever gonna get to go back to Evoque? Never. Dude, we need to do this right."

Leif knew there was no point in arguing. He sighed. "Fine. But let me get your pussy-for-rent mask right." He pressed it to Jamie's face again and marked the eye holes and pinched the nose and molded it for a perfect fit. "So, do you want sexy kitty, stylish kitty, or slutty kitty?"

Jamie grinned.

"Right," Leif replied. "Slutty kitty it is."

CHAPTER THREE

RUSS'S MOOD hadn't improved. As the masquerade ball crept closer—it was just two days away now—he tried to garner some excitement, but he couldn't quite manage it.

Because every day closer to the masquerade ball meant another day closer to Christmas. The charity ball was on the fifteenth. The twenty-fifth would follow soon enough. He seriously considered leaving town, leaving the country even. A beach in the tropics sounded like a great idea. Where no one knew him, and he could be anyone he wanted. He could find some holiday fling, some guy to have dinner with and pretend to be happy . . .

And somehow, that was more depressing.

Caleb came into his office holding a white box. "It's here," he said.

Russ closed his laptop. He didn't want Caleb to see him doing internet searches for tropical escape holidays.

"Here is what, exactly?" Russ asked.

"Your mask." Caleb put the white box on the desk and grinned. "Open it and tell me I don't have impeccable taste."

Russ opened the box. Nestled safely inside was a black-and-silver mask. Well, the face part was black, but the decorative part was silver. It looked kind of Roman or Grecian, with a crest of some kind standing high on the forehead and a Pegasus on either side of it. It was intricate but looked durable. Actually, it looked real. As though it was from Roman times. As though it would be heavy and like it cost a small fortune.

"It's ah . . . it's . . . It's not Christmassy."

Caleb tried to hide his disappointment, but Russ saw it clear enough. "You don't like it?"

"No, I do. Actually, I kind of really like it," Russ replied. He smiled and lifted it out of the box. It wasn't as heavy as it looked, but it was sturdy and very well made. "It's beautiful."

Caleb sighed with relief. "Oh, thank God." Then he launched into the finer details. "It started as a Perseus design, but I asked for extra pizzazz. And no, it's not Christmassy but neither are you, and if I produced anything remotely garish, you'd refuse point-blank." He gave an apologetic shrug, though Russ wasn't offended at all because Caleb was one hundred percent correct. "Anyway, it's handmade, of course. One of a kind. It's a little longer in the face, so once you get there and are wearing it, no one will know who you are."

Russ looked at him, his gaze narrowed and expression wary. "Why don't I want people to know who I am?" Russ didn't want to blow his own trumpet, but almost everyone knew who he was, especially in Evoque.

Caleb gave him his *must I spell it out for you?* look. "So you can let your hair down. Be yourself, have some fun without every set of eyes watching your every move." His whole face softened. "You need this, Russ. You can make your speech and welcome everyone, thank them all for attending, blah blah blah. Then we do a quick wardrobe change in your office and you're free to be as anonymous as you want."

Complete anonymity.

Russ had to admit . . . he liked the sound of that.

Could he shed his skin for a night? Could he be one of the crowd and maybe have a few drinks and dance with some guys without it being declared a national incident?

Well, maybe not a national incident. But a big enough incident in Vintage Ridge for it to reach the real-estate community and the business and financial fraternity, so when he went to work meetings or appointments on Monday, there'd be whispers and shared photos on the internet.

Yeah. Russ could use some anonymity.

"If you wanted to get a little festive, I thought perhaps we could accessorize, but I didn't want to push my luck."

Russ almost laughed. "You know me well."

Caleb grinned. "Thank you."

"And what will you be wearing?" Russ asked.

Caleb offered a smug smile. "It's a surprise. But just so you know, you did mention a naughty elf and it gave me an idea, and I will be putting the *ho* back into Ho Ho Ho."

Russ chuckled. "Please don't get arrested."

Caleb winked. "But they bring the handcuffs." Then he brightened. "Oh, speaking of which, have you been to Ace's Wild yet?"

"No, not yet. I've been busy." Which was true. He had been busy. He was always busy.

"Make sure you do." Caleb closed the box with the mask in it. "Masks I can order. Props and sex toys, not so much."

Russ snorted. "Yeah, I can manage that, thanks."

"Good." Caleb checked his watch, back to professional now. "You have an appointment at two with the interior design hopefuls for the warehouse loft, and given you haven't eaten yet and more than likely won't and you'll be here late, I've taken the liberty to order you something. It'll be here shortly."

Russ sighed. "What would I do without you?"

"Starve to death, miss every appointment and meeting—ever. Not pay any bills or know when your real-estate lawyers are—"

Russ put his hand up. "It was supposed to be rhetorical, but yes. You're probably right."

Caleb smiled, his chin raised a fraction higher as he walked out.

THE INTERIOR DESIGNERS were everything Russ expected.

Sharp, tidy, predictable.

Mediocre.

The warehouse was a huge space close to the center of the city. Once upon a time, the warehouse district had been the industrial part of town, the epicenter of industry and transport, storage and smaller production factories. Now it was a real-estate gold mine.

Correction.

Now it was Russ's real-estate gold mine.

With a sound working knowledge of building codes and zoning restrictions and the financial collateral to back the project, Russ had secured quite a few landmark warehouses. The legal battle was over, the zoning and building codes all straightened out, and the green light had been given to proceed with his next real-estate project.

Structural engineers had done their part, architects had done theirs. Russ had overseen every step, as he did with all projects, and construction had begun. There were already a few coffee shops and cafés beginning to sprout in the area, and the warehouse district was now pegged to be the next boom.

Because that was what Russ Quarrington did. He bought, developed, built, remodeled, renovated, and re-sold. He read markets, saw opportunities, and profited.

He'd found a warehouse with a great loft space and he wanted to remodel it and possibly live in it. He wanted an interior designer with edge and vision. He didn't want someone who aspired to be on some reality TV house-flip show. He wanted someone who thought outside the box. Someone who dared to be bold and make a statement with their art.

He didn't want to pay someone from New York to come down. He wanted to keep the business in Vintage Ridge without sacrificing his taste or integrity.

Russ was very well aware that most businesses slowed down in the holidays. Winter dragged its sorry ass through productivity and inspiration, but the hopeful designers and the usual suspects just weren't up for the job.

Or, Russ reasoned, maybe he shouldn't be making decisions while he was in this funk. Maybe the issue was with him and not the interior designers. Maybe nothing felt right because *he* didn't feel right.

At least Russ could compartmentalize and acknowledge the issue might have been him. So he had Caleb advise all designers that no decisions would be made until the new year. Surely his morose outlook on every single thing would be lifted by the new year.

Surely.

"Okay, you're coming with me," Caleb said.

Russ startled, shooting him a confused look. "What?"

"I've been having a one-sided conversation for five minutes apparently. You keep staring out the window like those dark gray clouds have offended you." Caleb was sitting opposite him, though Russ hadn't even known he'd come into his office at all. His smile was sad and sorry. "I know it hasn't been easy this year. I mean, the holidays are rough every year, but this year feels different. It feels heavier."

"It does," Russ agreed quietly. "I don't know why."

"I want you to come with me," Caleb said. "You can take the rest of the afternoon off. There's nothing that won't wait until tomorrow."

Russ's frown became a scowl. "Where are we going?"

"Out of this office. You need a change of scenery, even if it's just for the afternoon." Caleb stood up and motioned for Russ to do the same. "Come along now. I'll drive."

Russ shut down his laptop and collected his wallet, keys, phone, and jacket, and followed Caleb to the elevator. "Any clues as to where you're taking me?"

"Absolutely not. Because then you wouldn't come with me."

"You're not instilling a great deal of confidence, just so you know."

Russ grumbled the whole way to the underground parking lot. Caleb unlocked his car, opened the door, but stared at Russ over the roof. "I mean this with the utmost respect, given you're my boss and all, and I truly do consider you to be a friend—" He put his hand over his heart. "—but for the love of God, will you just get in and stop whining? I know you don't like Christmas, but it's one of my most favorite times of year, so please, please, please stop pissing on my parade."

Russ stared, openmouthed, and Caleb grinned and got in behind the wheel.

Pouting, Russ got in. He was just about to gripe that they weren't taking his car, but Caleb was right. Russ's mood was affecting those around him. So instead, he sighed. "Can I at least get a hint about where we're going?"

Caleb drove up out of the underground parking lot to the gloomy December daylight, stopped at the barrier gate, and grinned. "We're going Christmas shopping."

Russ felt as though he'd entered some weird alternative universe. "Christmas what?"

"It's sixteen days till Christmas," Caleb explained, driving out onto the street. "I usually take care of all office Christmas gifts for clients and business associates, but this year you can help."

Oh, dear God. This wasn't some weird dimensional universe shit. This was hell on earth.

"And then," Caleb said, even cheerier than before, "we're going to see Ace and Wilder at the sex-toy shop. You need a prop of some kind to go with that kickass mask."

CHAPTER FOUR

LEIF HEARD Jamie's laughter coming from the back of the house, followed by his trudging footsteps toward the workshop. He smiled as he added the final spray of color to his mask, and the doors opened.

Jamie let himself in, fighting with the heavy old door in the cold wind, cussing at it under his breath before he got it closed, turned around, and straightened up. "Your mom said you were out here . . ." His voice trailed off when he saw what Leif was working on. "Holy shit."

Leif chuckled. "It's not finished yet."

"It's . . . it's huge!"

"Do you like it?"

"Are you kidding me? It's fucking awesome!" He stood beside Leif, staring at the 'mask', and grinned. "You wanna hope Evoque has tall doorways because you're already six foot one. This is gonna make you seven-something foot tall."

Leif chuckled. "It is kinda big. I'll just carry it in and put it on when I get inside."

"And what?" Jamie asked, puzzled. "Ruin your chance

at a grand entrance? Hell no. Wear it in, and duck if you have to."

Leif considered that, then turned the mask, which was really more of a headpiece than mask, and eyed it over. It was currently braced on an upturned jar, helping keep its shape. He was happy with how it had turned out. He'd begun with a mask piece, added a structured headband for support, and added two decent-sized twigs as antlers. He'd sanded, sculpted, primed, positioned, fastened, and secured. Each antler was almost a foot long, with smaller offshoots giving them an authentic look, and he'd just finished painting them matte black. They looked almost like wrought iron, and tomorrow he would add the silver leaves and feathers to the headband and mask. "I need to add some final touches when the paint dries. I can't do much else with it today."

Jamie gave him a shit-eating grin. "You are gonna be the sexiest fucking Rudolph the Reindeer ever. Well, if Rudolph was the lovechild of Maleficent and Puck from *A Midsummer Night's Dream*, and they had sex on a wrought iron chandelier."

Leif laughed. "Perfect. But I'm not wearing a red nose, so you can forget about that."

Jamie laughed and whacked Leif with the back of his hand. "You won't need it. You're gonna look amazing."

"Do you wanna see your finished mask?"

His face lit up. "You finished it already?"

Leif opened the box he'd put it in and pulled out the finished mask. He'd added cat ears and more thin braids of leather to the fastener at the back. He'd wanted his very own cat-o'-nine-tails, and that was exactly what Leif had given him. All those scraps and offcuts of leather had finally come in handy. He'd had to mix and match, splice and tie odd strands together so the strands were different colors, different widths, different lengths, and different kinds of leather: some soft, some not so soft. But it really did add to the charm of it.

"Oh, Leif," he murmured, holding it, feeling it, smelling it. He put it to his face without tying it off, and yeah, it fit just fine. "It's beautiful."

"It kind of makes you look like Rum Tum Tugger from *Cats*."

Jamie purred, batted his eyelashes, and pretended to swish a nonexistent tail. "Meee-oww," he drawled, making Leif laugh. "It's perfect! Thank you!"

"You're welcome. It was fun to make."

He popped it back into its box and closed the lid. "Righto. Grab your coat, Rudolph. Or we'll run out of time. I'm working a double shift tomorrow, so we have to do this today."

"Okay, okay," Leif said, slipping his coat on. The masquerade gala was just two days away. "And you're sure we need to go to this store in particular?"

Jamie gave him a cheeky smirk. "Oh, I'm sure."

A short while later, Jamie pulled into a parking lot next to a brick building with white trim. It looked built in the 50s, but cute and welcoming. It certainly didn't overtly look like a sex-toy store, but the stylized handcuffs in the sign proudly proclaiming *Ace's Wild*, were telling. Even though Leif had never set foot inside the store, he'd heard of the owners. They were icons in the gay community in Vintage Ridge. Ace and Wilder were an older interracial couple who'd grown up locally but spent much of their younger years traveling the US where they'd championed LGBTQ+ equality. Now they were back in Vintage Ridge, and there wasn't a gay soul in town who didn't know who Ace and Wilder were.

"And this is my treat, remember," Jamie said as they got out of his car.

"I don't expect you to pay for anything for me," Leif tried to object.

"You saved me money on the mask. And before you can lecture me on what saving money actually means, I'm doing this for you, so shut up. Consider it a Christmas present if you want."

Leif gave up arguing and held the door to the store open for him instead. Jamie walked in and stopped. "Though I should probably put down a disclaimer that we're after accessories. If you want a sex sling or a St. Andrew's cross, you can pay for that."

Leif chuckled again, taking in the rows and rows of different items. They were greeted by a tall, buff man behind the counter. He wore jeans and a retro T-shirt, his mature locs were tied back, and he had kind eyes and a warm, wide smile. "Good afternoon, gentlemen!" he said, his voice a rich baritone. "And welcome to Ace's Wild. Is there anything we can help you boys with today?"

God, did he just want us to yell out that we're here for sex props? In front of other customers? Leif was trying to think of what to say when Jamie replied first. "We're just looking for the moment," Jamie said. "But thanks."

A shorter guy, impeccably dressed in trousers and a vest, with neat blond hair and wire-rimmed glasses, joined him behind the counter. "Ace, leave the first-timers alone," he said, swatting the taller guy on the arm. He had a mischievous smile, and he winked at Leif and Jamie. "You two wander and look around, and I'll come find you in a minute."

"Thanks," Jamie replied brightly.

First-timers? "I think he thinks we're a couple," Leif whispered as they ventured down the first aisle.

Jamie picked up a pack of glow-in-the-dark condoms, completely unfazed. "He wouldn't be the first."

Leif sighed and conceded a nod. That was true. A lot of people thought that, but Jamie was like a brother to Leif and vice versa. They'd practiced kissing in junior high, and they'd tried to level-up to mutual hand jobs, but it was weird. Leif had felt like he was about to jerk one of his brothers off, and Jamie had sagged with relief when Leif had called the experiment off. It was weird for him too, and they'd never entertained the notion again. They were best friends, brothers even. Inseparable, but never lovers.

"Would you ever get a Prince Albert?" Jamie asked, taking some package off the wall and inspecting it.

"Nope. Would you?"

"Hell no. Would I let a guy with a Prince Albert fuck me? Hell yes, I would."

Leif snorted and they moved on to the cock rings, butt plugs, Fleshlights and fake asses, and every kind of anal wand there was. Jamie dragged him over to the dildo section, where he contemplated every single kind: wearable, attachable, vibrating, strap-on, and the double-edged kinds. "Oh look, the Darth Maul lightsaber of dildos."

Leif burst out laughing and quickly looked around, hoping he wasn't disturbing the other customers. There were another two men together, perhaps a couple, one woman and one man, but no one even looked up.

"These are hardly props for our costumes," Leif added as he considered one particularly extra-large dildo. Christ almighty. Just looking at it made his butthole clench.

"Mmm," Jamie said, eyeing the same dildo. "Now we're

talking . . ." He picked it up and slapped his palm heavily with it. "Could have some fun with this."

He looked at his friend like he'd lost his mind. "Could also have a prolapsed ass or possibly some internal organ rearrangement."

Jamie laughed and put it back on the shelf. "Where's your sense of adventure?"

"Nowhere near monster cocks, that's where." He nodded toward the next aisle. "That's more what I'm after."

Jamie's grin widened, and he nudged Leif with his elbow. "You kinky fucker."

Leif nudged him right back. "Says the guy who likes to have his liver prodded by monster cocks." Jamie burst out laughing, so Leif left him to it and went to the next aisle.

Yes, this was exactly what he had in mind. The aisle was full of collars and cuffs, and there were harnesses at the end and on the far wall. He'd considered getting a harness or even trying to make one, but he wanted his mask and headpiece to be the feature.

And in keeping with his reindeer theme, being an animal and all, a collar was a more fitting choice. And Leif would be lying if he said he didn't like the idea of wearing a collar, and this really was the best excuse to wear one . . .

He slid a thinner one off the hook and inspected the craftsmanship. It was good, and the clasp was quality, but it wouldn't gel with the proportion of his antlers . . .

So he selected a thicker one. It was black leather, maybe two inches wide, with a quality clasp and a separate O-ring. It was sturdy but soft and wouldn't be uncomfortable at all if he wore it for a few hours. He checked the price and smiled. It wasn't ridiculously expensive, thank God.

"You like that one," a deep voice said beside him. It was the guy from behind the counter . . . even without introductions, Leif knew his name was Ace. "You have good taste. Is it for yourself or your partner?" He nodded to where Jamie was now looking at floggers.

"It's for a costume design," Leif replied. He didn't want anyone to think he wore collars, even if he rather liked the idea. "But yeah, it's for me. And he's not my partner. Just a friend."

Ace smiled, a knowing sparkle in his eye; then he studied Leif's neck. "Well, you have the bone structure for the wider collar. Tall, long neck. Try it on."

Leif figured testing it was a good idea, so he took off his coat and dropped it at his feet, unclasped the collar, and slid it around his neck, though his nerves got the better of him and he struggled getting it cinched back up.

"Here, let me," Ace said. He deftly redid the buckle, smiling ever so slightly. He was fiftyish, well-built, and ruggedly gorgeous. Leif felt like a kid having his necktie straightened by a grown-up. And, most disturbingly, Leif liked how that felt.

"Oh yeah," Ace said; his voice rumbled. "It was made for you. And I ain't just saying that. Take a look." He nodded to the mirror halfway down the aisle.

Leif walked to it and saw his reflection. And yeah . . . it suited him.

But not just that. He stood a little taller, held his head a little higher, and felt a little warmer all over.

Yeah, he liked it a lot.

It sat comfortably around his neck, from the beginning of his collarbones to just under his jaw.

"How does that feel?" Ace asked.

Leif nodded, his movement somewhat restricted. "Feels good."

Ace grinned and gave him a few pointers about fit and

movement, wear, and leather-care. "Holy shit, Leif," Jamie said, walking up the aisle toward them. "That's really hot. And with your antlers, well damn . . . a little kitty like me won't even get noticed."

"Antlers?" Ace asked.

"Oh, I made a thing," Leif said, motioning above his head. "For the masquerade gala."

"At Evoque?" Ace whispered, looking around the shop. He spotted two guys at the service counter and whispered even quieter. "Just between us, guys. The man in the blue coat? That's Russ Quarrington."

Leif and Jamie both shot a glance toward the front of the store. "*The* Russ Quarrington?" Leif whispered. Russ Quarrington, prominent real-estate mogul, who owned half of Vintage Ridge.

Ace nodded, and the three of them watched as Russ Quarrington and the man he was with finalized their purchase and headed toward the door. The other guy was smaller but very well dressed and hadn't stopped talking or smiling yet. He used his hands to talk and was kind of cute. Leif didn't get a great look at Quarrington's face before they disappeared out the door, but he had short, well-styled brown hair and a coat that probably cost what Leif might make in six months. He seemed serious, and maybe that came with being one of Vintage Ridge's richest men. Though he seemed younger than Leif might have assumed.

Not that it made any difference to Leif. He'd rather be broke and happy than rich and miserable. Sure, money'd be nice, but not if it cost him his soul.

"I don't think we have to worry about crossing paths with him at the gala," Leif said. "We're not his type."

"And what type is that?" Ace asked.

"Poor," Jamie answered, and Leif laughed. He wasn't exactly wrong.

Ace smiled. "Nah, I've met Mr. Quarrington a few times now. He's a decent man. Quiet, keeps to himself, but surprisingly, he's down to earth. He's a nice guy."

"I guess," Leif conceded. He didn't like to judge anyone, especially for their financial status, but the man was reportedly worth several million dollars, and Leif couldn't quite grasp that amount of wealth. "The gala's for charity, so he can't be too bad."

Ace gave him a warm smile that was genuine, and although Leif didn't know him, he liked him. "So, if you have antlers, what kind of buck are you?"

"Reindeer. You know, being Christmas and all."

Ace laughed. "Nice. And what are you going as?" he asked Jamie.

"I'm a Christmas kitty," Jamie said. He held up a boxed dildo Leif hadn't realized he was holding. "I really like your range of cat toys, by the way."

Ace's low rumbling laughter boomed in the shop. "We do aim to please." The shorter salesman joined them, and Ace put his arm around his shoulder and had him face Jamie. "Wilder, my love. Could you please be so kind as to show this little Christmas kitty where he might find some *actual* kitty toys."

Wilder didn't even blink, as though shit like this was an everyday occurrence. He took Jamie by the arm and led him away, over to what looked like a display of crops. Leif smiled as they walked away. "I would apologize for him, but I'm not entirely sorry."

Ace chuckled again. "I like you, kid."

"You called that man Wilder? You called him 'my love'? Is he your partner?" Leif knew this—everyone knew who they were—but it felt weirdly intrusive to assume, so he posed it as a question.

"Husband. We've been together longer than you've had years." Ace watched Wilder with such affection, with such love, Leif felt as though he'd intruded.

"Wow, that's . . . amazing. You're lucky to find that." Leif cleared his throat and was reminded that he was still wearing the collar. He began to take it off, but Ace stopped him.

"Here, let me get that."

"Oh, um . . ." Leif felt his cheeks heat. "Feel like I'm going to prom all over again and my mom is fixing my tie." And that was saying something because Leif had been taller than his mom and brothers by the time he was fourteen.

Ace beamed, and when he'd unclasped the collar, he handed it back to Leif. "The Evoque Masquerade Gala's better than prom though, right?"

"Oh sure," Leif replied. "I'm really excited, even though I have no idea what to expect."

"A lot of hot men and sexy women, cocktails, music, and mystery masks," Ace answered.

"Have you been?"

"To Evoque? Plenty of times, but never to the gala. Man, those tickets are exclusive and expensive. How'd you score two of 'em?"

"Jamie won them online. We certainly wouldn't be going otherwise. I'm an industrial-art student at the community college, and Jamie's studying sociology during the day and he busses tables at a restaurant downtown when he can. Not exactly high-life, but we get by."

"Well, you're gonna have a night to remember!" Ace said warmly. "And you know what every good collar needs?"

"Um," Leif blushed again. "No, not really. I haven't done this before."

Ace held his gaze. "But you like it," he said, low enough so only Leif could hear. "I saw that look in your eyes and your smile when you first tried it on."

"Uh, yeah. I always wondered . . ."

"There's no shame in it," Ace said adamantly. "In fact, it's a beautiful thing."

"Beautiful?"

Ace made a happy sound. "Mm, hell yes. And believe me when I say this—I've been on both ends of a collar—it's beautiful."

"Both ends?"

Ace grinned and took a long leather strand off the display wall, and when Ace undid the eye clasp at one end, the handle at the other, Leif could see what it was. "Yes, boy. Because don't you know? Every collar needs a leash."

CHAPTER FIVE

THE GALA NIGHT couldn't come quick enough. Russ just wanted it to be over. Because then it would be just two weeks till Christmas was over, and this shitty time of the year could be over and done with. He was loath to spend another Christmas alone—like this one was shaping up, just like all the lonely Christmases he'd spent alone in the last sixteen years.

He just wanted it to all be over. And he was even more determined to book a few days away, including the twenty-fifth of December, to some tropical beach where he could unwind, relax, and pretend there wasn't a gaping hole where his family used to be.

Fuck, he hated Christmas.

Mexico would be nice this time of year. No . . . Argentina or Brazil.

But first, he just needed to get through this night. One small speech to welcome everyone, then he could change outfits, put on a face mask, and be someone else for a night.

The crowd began to arrive right on time, and Russ showed his face, welcoming the earlier guests personally. It wasn't a complete chore; he enjoyed the charity gala night every year. It was for a good cause. For some reason, this year he was feeling less festive than any other.

"Here." Caleb shoved a drink in his hand. "Your fake smile is painful to watch."

"My fake smile?"

Caleb raised an eyebrow. "The one you've been wearing since the first guests arrived. The same one you wear in meetings with people you can't stand. No one else can probably tell the difference, but I can. Please have one drink. Loosen up a little."

"Caleb," he began.

"Every single thing is taken care of. You have nothing to worry about, except your welcome speech. Then we'll change your jacket, put on your mask, and you can see if there's anyone who interests you."

"Yeah, right," Russ said, taking a long drink of his scotch. "I've seen all that Vintage Ridge has to offer."

"And that's why I got you the mask," Caleb said. "So you can enjoy some secrecy. Some fun, some mystery and excitement."

"You make it sound like a Scooby Doo movie."

Caleb smiled at that. "Can I be Fred?"

"Hell no. You're Velma." Caleb's expression was horrified, so Russ explained. "I mean, because you're the smart one, the one who figures everything out. I'm Fred," Russ said, his hand to his chest. "Thinks he's the shit but he's actually kind of stupid."

Caleb rolled his eyes. "You're not stupid. And I'm not Velma. I would never *ever* wear orange on orange. Ever. At least let me be Daphne."

Russ finally managed a laugh and by the time he was due to make his welcoming speech, almost all guests had arrived. The nightclub lights were dimmed, the music stopped, and everyone turned to the stage. There was a range of masks. Some traditional, a few *Phantom of the Opera* style, a few steampunk, a couple of Zorro's, a few goth crows and owls, a few artsy ones, which Russ had to admit looked really awesome. The guests had really stepped up this year, and instead of a standard masquerade ball, it was more couture, more cosplay. Every year the outfits got better and better.

Russ gave his speech, he thanked everyone for attending and for helping raise money for such a good cause. But Russ knew better than anyone that no one really cared for speeches. No one really wanted to hear sponsors drone on. They were here to party and have a good night, so with a raise of his champagne glass, he bid everyone a great night. People clapped and the music began again, and Russ smiled his way through the crowd to his office. Caleb was a step behind him and, in no time had Russ's blue suit coat off and was helping him into a tight-fitting leather coat. It had a high neck cowl, a zipper that ran from his right shoulder to the left side of his waist. Paired with black jeans and biker boots, Caleb had said it was some *Assassin's Creed*-inspired thing, and he wasn't fucking wrong.

"I look stupid."

"You look hot." Caleb was admiring his masterpiece, tugging at the collar a little and fixing a sleeve. "And no one will recognize you in this, and that's the whole point, right?"

Russ grumbled a noncommittal reply; arguing at this stage was pointless.

Caleb held up the mask. "And for the pièce de résistance."

Once Russ had the mask on, he realized Caleb was staring. "Do I look as ridiculous as I feel?"

"No, I—" He shook his head. "—never really appreciated *Assassin's Creed* until this moment. You look sexy as fuck and completely unrecognizable."

"Oh. So I'm not sexy when I'm recognizable?"

Caleb snorted. "Not to me, no. You know you're not my type."

Russ laughed because he knew that very well. Caleb's type was the gym-junkie, quarterback type, which Russ certainly was not. And he appreciated Caleb's blunt honesty. "What about you? Where's your mask?"

He peeled out of his coat and then his shirt. Wearing only pants, he went to his bag of goodies, and he slipped on a brown leather harness, fixed on some pointed ear-tips with astonishing precision, then fitted a felt Christmas elf hat. He whipped off his suit pants to reveal striped tights underneath and put on some hideous elf shoes with bells on them.

Jesus Christ. Russ was flabbergasted, a little horrified, and duly impressed.

"How do I look?" Caleb asked. His wide-eyed innocence was an evil ruse.

"If the Grinch ever did porn," Russ replied. "That's how you look."

Caleb beamed. "Perfect." Then he stopped. "Oh, almost forgot." He reached back into the bag and pulled out what they'd gone to Ace's Wild to get. A thigh holster for a tall bottle of lube and a foil strip of condoms, which Caleb strapped to Russ's thigh.

"Christ," Russ grumbled. "I'm gonna get arrested for impersonating a SWAT cop, and you're gonna get arrested for prostitution."

Caleb gasped, faking offense. "It's only prostitution if they give me money, and believe me, I happily do this for free. Now come on, you're missing your own party."

They snuck back out and slipped into the crowd. There were more people here now, the dance floor was full, the music was loud, and everyone looked amazing. They got a drink each and made their way to the upstairs platform so they could see everyone.

And no one seemed to pay him any attention. Well, they looked with clear appreciation, but not because they knew it was Russ Quarrington. Caleb, on the other hand, got a lot of attention, blatantly interested looks and playful smiles, which he lapped up and reveled in. "You should go and mingle," Russ told him, having to lean in over the music. "Put some of those guys out of their misery."

Caleb sipped his drink. "Not yet. You need another drink first, then you can go mingle too."

"I'm fine," Russ said, scanning the groups of guys nearby. Even with masks on, he was certain he'd seen them all here before. "Not sure I'll be staying long anyway."

"Why not?"

Russ turned his back to the dance floor and bar, leaned against the railing, and sipped his drink. "Thanks for the outfit and the mask. It was a nice idea, but I don't think I'll find what I'm looking for here tonight."

"Oh really?"

"Yeah. I appreciate what you did, but these are the same faces. Even under the masks."

Caleb, still facing the crowd, smiled. "Maybe not. Turn around."

Russ turned, and he didn't have to ask Caleb who he was referring to. Because in the middle of the crowd, heading toward the bar, was a man Russ was certain he'd never seen before.

He'd never seen anything like him before.

He was tall, wearing black jeans and no shirt. His lean

torso was milky white under the black light, but the most remarkable thing was on his head. He wore huge black antlers, which made him look incredibly tall, with a black mask over his eyes, and fucking hell . . . he was wearing a thick black collar. People made a path for him to walk, like the parting of the Red Sea.

He was graceful, gorgeous, and utterly striking. Russ couldn't look away and neither could anyone else in the nightclub.

"Do you think they're together?" Caleb asked.

"Who?"

"Rocky and Bullwinkle."

"What?"

"The guy who's with the antler-guy."

Russ hadn't even noticed anyone with him . . . He hadn't taken his eyes off the antler-guy. "He's um . . . he's . . . wow."

Caleb didn't reply and Russ could feel him staring, so he finally dragged his eyes off the antler-guy to meet Caleb's gaze. He was smiling at him under that mask with those pointy ears.

"What?"

"That's the first time I've ever seen you look like that at a guy."

Russ shook his head but his eyes went straight back down to the antler-guy. "He's beautiful."

"Come on," Caleb said, taking Russ's arm.

"Where are we going?" he hissed.

Caleb stopped at the top of the short flight of stairs that led down to the main floor area. "You're going to put your-self out there," he said. "Complete anonymity, remember. You have nothing to lose."

Nothing to lose . . . right. Just my dignity.

But Caleb pulled him down the stairs and into the crowded floor area. The crowd was drinking and dancing, talking and laughing. But they were also eyeing everyone else, seeing who had the better mask, the better costume. Russ could feel eyes on him now, and he wondered if they knew it was him. Apparently quite a few men liked the *Assassin's Creed* look.

Or maybe they were more interested in the slutty elf he was with. Caleb's tights didn't exactly leave much to the imagination . . . By the time they got to the bar, Russ had convinced himself they were looking at Caleb.

Caleb just slid in right next to the antler-guy at the bar, who was even more spectacular close up.

He was taller than Russ, maybe an inch or two, but his antlers made him over seven feet tall. There were silver leaves and feathers at the headband, as though he was from some magical fairyland, but the antlers were black and surreal; the whole thing looked as though it was made from metal. His eye mask was simple black leather because the true art piece was on his head. There was blond hair underneath, and Russ was sure he had blue eyes. Though he was trying not to stare . . . it wasn't easy.

The thick collar around his neck was simple and stunning, and Russ could see now it had a thin leash clipped to the front of it. The handle of the leash went from his throat to around his wrist, like a leather jewelry piece. His pale skin shimmered under the neon lights. Not overly muscled, but firm and lean, his nipples pink, a faint trail of hair ran from his navel to underneath the waistband of his jeans.

Black jeans, slung low, showcasing what lay beneath. A warm shiver ran through Russ when he thought about what that bulge might mean.

He was the most beautiful man Russ had ever seen.

"Hello? Anybody home?" Caleb said, giving him a nudge before handing him another drink.

Russ had to make himself look away, turning to Caleb. "Sorry, I just . . ." He looked back to the guy with antlers. *Fuck, Russ wanted him.*

"I think your boyfriend has a thing for reindeer," a voice said.

Russ turned then to see the man the antler-guy was with speaking to Caleb. There was no malice in his tone, just a playful smile. He had a set of cat ears on with long leather braids over his shoulder down his front. He was shirtless and wearing a harness, much like Caleb's, and he was holding a crop that had a bell and a feather on it. Like a cat toy but also for spanking.

"Oh, he's not my boyfriend," Caleb said, moving in closer to the cat-guy. "Though your reindeer boyfriend cuts one helluva figure."

The cat-guy gently booped Caleb on the nose with his cat toy, grinning. "Silly elf, he's not my boyfriend either."

"Well, cute kitty cat, I'm glad we cleared that mess up right away."

The kitty cat smiled, all seductive like, and just like that, in less than thirty seconds and the briefest conversation ever, Caleb had picked up.

Christ.

Caleb pulled Russ over and said, "This is my friend Ru . . . Rogue."

Kitty-cat guy waved his hand at his friend. "And this is . . . Rudolph."

Russ felt like he was in high school all over again. "Uh, hi," he said, awkwardly. "Can I get a round of drinks?"

They'd just gotten drinks, being at the bar and all, but

the kitty-cat guy waved his cat toy prop, making the bell jingle. "Yes, please."

Russ smiled and ordered their drinks. The barman looked twice at him, clearly seeing who it was underneath the mask, or maybe he caught a glimpse of his wallet and ID . . . God, so much for anonymity. But he never said anything. Just gave a sly wink and a smile as he handed him his change.

Once they'd got their drinks, they moved away from the bar and found a quieter, less crowded corner. Kitty cat and Caleb were all smiles and quiet chatter, standing close together, their hands on each other's arms. And that left Russ and . . . Rudolph.

"Your antlers are amazing," Russ said. He let out a flustered breath. "And the collar . . ."

Rudolph smiled slowly. "And the collar, what?"

Russ chewed on his bottom lip and looked him right in the eyes. "It's hot. Never really thought collars were my thing, until now."

Rudolph's smile widened. "Me either. And thanks. I made the antlers myself. And the mask."

Russ couldn't hide his surprise. "You're clearly very—" He was going to say 'good with your hands' but stopped himself. "Talented."

Rudolph laughed. "Thanks for the drink."

"You're welcome. And I like the leash," Russ said, lightly touching it. The way he had it slipped around his wrist, the way the metal clip joined to his collar. "It's a nice touch."

"I was going to make a bridle," he replied with a smirk. "But thought it might be a bit too much."

Russ laughed. "Maybe. Or maybe not." He met

Rudolph's gaze again. "I think the collar's perfect. The whole outfit, actually."

He smiled, and those flawless pink lips curved upward deliciously. "And your outfit is very cool. Love the jacket. I'm trying to decide if you look like a superhero or a villain."

Russ shrugged. "Maybe a little of both."

His kitty-cat friend interrupted, telling them both. "We're going to dance."

Caleb smiled and, holding the leather braids in his hand, let them run over the kitty's shoulder. "We might be a while, so *you*"—he looked pointedly at Russ—"can have some fun."

Rudolph smiled after his friend, looked back at Russ, and laughed. "I hope your friend can handle trouble."

Russ chuckled. "He can give as good as he gets."

He leaned in so they could speak over the music. "He wants you to have fun? So, you need help with that?"

"I work a lot," Russ replied, explaining hopefully enough.

Just then, another guy—who Russ knew ran an accounting firm in town and he'd seen at the club before but who clearly didn't recognize Russ in his costume—approached Rudolph, looking him up and down. Russ could guess it was supposed to be sexy, but it came off as sleazy and intrusive. "You looking for a man to hold your leash?" the guy said.

Jesus. Was that supposed to be a come-on?

Rudolph stared him right in the eye for a full three seconds before answering. Totally composed, confident. "Well, I was working on it, but you interrupted."

Oh. Russ couldn't help but smile. The man gave a brief glance to Russ but turned back to Rudolph. "If you need—"

"No." Rudolph's reply wasn't aggressive at all, simply

clear and concise. "I decide who I give my leash to. No one else."

The guy opened his mouth to speak again, his stupid Batman mask slipping a little, and Russ lost all patience for him. Not here, not in his club, and not with him. "He said no," Russ said, his voice low and final. "If you need a lesson in consent, I'll be glad to give it to you."

The idiot had the audacity to look offended, but he took the hint and with a grunt and a sneer, he walked away. Thankfully Russ didn't have to get security involved.

"Well, that guy was a dick," Rudolph said.

"He was."

"Do you give lessons in consent often?" He smirked behind his glass as he took a sip.

"Only when required," Russ said with a smile. He wasn't misreading this. Rudolph was definitely interested. Russ finished his drink and nodded toward Rudolph's half-empty glass. "Can I get you another one?"

He smiled, and there was heat in his eyes. They were a fiery blue behind his mask. Then without breaking eye contact, he downed the rest of his drink and held the glass out to Russ. "Sure."

Russ took the glass, his hand lingering for a beat too long. "Or should we dance first?"

Rudolph grinned. "We should totally dance first."

CHAPTER SIX

LEIF WAS ALREADY A LITTLE TIPSY. He'd had two drinks pretty quickly and he didn't drink often, so the buzz he had going on gave him the courage he might not have normally had. He took Rogue's hand—though he highly doubted Rogue was his real name—and led him through the crowd. The thing about being tall and then having another foot of antlers was that people moved and gave them room on the dance floor.

Rogue was sexy, no doubt about it. Not that Leif could see much of him. His coat and cowl covered up to his chin, his mask was well-fitted, but Leif could see his hazel eyes well enough. He had full lips that were made for kissing, and he was the perfect kissing height; a little shorter than Leif, so if Leif tilted Rogue's chin up a fraction, he could kiss him perfectly.

He wanted to.

But he had no clue who this man was. Was that half the appeal? Was the anonymity what made it so alluring?

Leif knew expensive leather when he saw it, and Rogue's coat spoke of money. It was possibly Italian, fitted perfectly, stitched to perfection. And it hugged his body like a glove. The kind of leather Leif could never afford, and maybe if they weren't wearing masks, Leif wouldn't stand a chance with a guy like this. So yeah, the mystery, the anonymity was great.

And it was just one night . . .

Leif put his hands to Rogue's waist and pulled him in so their bodies pressed together. Rogue grunted with the impact, his lips parting, his eyes alight with desire. And they began to dance, a slow, grinding, dirty dance. Not made easy by the mass of antlers on his head or the thick-banded collar around his neck, but the restrictions felt good.

Rogue slid his arms around Leif's back, and it felt so incredible, for a moment Leif had forgotten he was shirtless. But Rogue's warm hands on his skin heated him all the way through. Was he imagining this chemistry, or was it the two vodkas he'd had? Was it the masks and the mystery? Or was it the way Rogue held him, swayed with him, looked at him with such fire in his eyes . . .

And suddenly they were no longer dancing. They weren't in a crowded nightclub surrounded by a mass of people. There was no one else, no music blaring, nothing but the two of them. Leif put his hands to Rogue's jaw and kissed him.

And for the briefest moment, Rogue froze. Leif wondered if he'd blown it, misread it, overstepped. But then Rogue sighed and melted into him, into their kiss. He held Leif tighter and Leif tilted his head and deepened the kiss.

Their masks bumped, but Leif kissed him harder. Rogue held him closer, his fingers dug in, his arms strong, and they began to grind in a different kind of dance.

God, Leif wanted him. He wanted more. He wanted to

give him the end of his leash and hand himself over. He wanted to let go, lose himself, lose control.

And if he didn't stop this kiss, he was going to lose it on the dance floor.

Reluctantly, he ended the kiss and pressed Rogue's forehead to his. His eyes were closed underneath the mask, his lips wet and parted. He needed a little distance so he could get his thoughts in order but didn't want Rogue to go too far. "How about we get that drink?"

Rogue nodded, and this time he took Leif's hand and led him toward the bar. He ordered their drinks, and when they had them, he suggested going to the mezzanine that overlooked the main bar. It was quieter, more private, and there were seats and tables with a view of the dance floor.

They took the stairs and found seats next to each other, and Leif pointed to the crowd below. There was Jamie and the raunchy Christmas elf dancing and laughing and having a fabulous time together. "Double trouble, then."

"Looks like it," Rogue said warmly.

"How do you and the Christmas elf know each other?"

"We work together," he replied with a bit of a frown. Then he said, "And you and the kitten?"

Leif grinned. "You mean the crazy cat? He's been my best friend since we were in elementary."

"Is that a real whip down his back?"

"Well, the braided leather's real. I made it."

Rogue glanced up at the antlers. "You made both of them?"

"Uh, yeah," Leif replied. He sipped his drink. "It's what I do."

"You're a costume designer?"

"No," he answered, realizing now how what he'd said sounded. "I do industrial design."

Rogue seemed a little impressed. "Is that so?"

"Yeah. Well, I'm still studying it and I'm mostly self-taught. I have a workshop, kind of." He wasn't about to say that the workshop was his mom's old garage, but while they were playing fantasy, he could pretend. "I love what I do. It's why I get up every day, and it's my passion."

"Well, you're brilliant." Rogue reached up and gently touched the antler. "This is amazing. I can see it as a chandelier or a feature of wall art."

Leif almost laughed. "I don't know if it's that good."

"Well, admittedly I'm no art critic," Rogue replied. He put his hand on Leif's knee. "But I know what I like when I see it."

Leif slid his hand over Rogue's and linked their fingers. He slid his seat a little closer, their sides touching, their faces close. "Is that so?"

"God, yes. Tell me, why the antlers?"

"Well, for a start, it's a Christmas masquerade and I'm a reindeer."

Rogue grinned. "Not because your real name is Rudolph?"

Leif chuckled. "No, it's not my real name. But it was also kinda fitting."

"Fitting? How so?"

"Well, coming here." He gestured to the nightclub below.

Rogue frowned again. "Is there something wrong with here?"

"No, not at all," Leif replied quickly. "It's everything I imagined it would be."

"You've never been here before?"

"No, this is my first time. It's not the kind of place we'd

normally go. My friend won the tickets on some Instagram thing."

The frown was back. "Why wouldn't you come here?"

Because I'm broke. Because I grew up poor . . . "Because I'm an industrial-design student at a community college. Money isn't something we have a lot of."

Rogue took a long sip of his drink, though he didn't seem too happy with this development. Mystery and fantasy had lost some shine now that reality and truth had come out. Jesus, men like this were all the same. Leif pulled his hand away, but Rogue was quick to grab it.

"You said the name was fitting? What did you mean?"

"What difference does it make?" Leif gave him a tight smile.

"I want to know."

As much as Leif hated that his little slivers of truth had doused their spark, his reply to this question was the exact point he was trying to make. "Why is being a reindeer fitting? Because these are reindeer games, are they not?" He waved to the crowd, to the bar, to the whole fucking sham. "An exclusive club for the elite and invited few, while those who aren't allowed in, because they don't meet the financial requisites, aren't allowed to play."

Rogue was stunned, clearly, even offended. And Leif knew he'd hit his mark. God, the rich and privileged were so predictable. He must be horrified he'd just been kissing a guy who was so far beneath him.

"You know, I think I'll go," Leif said, standing up. "Thank you for the drinks and the dance."

Rogue grabbed his hand. "Wait! Don't go, please. Sit with me and talk. I want to hear what you have to say."

"About what?"

"About everything. Be honest with me. No one is ever honest with me and I need to hear it."

Leif almost laughed. "You're asking for honesty when we're wearing masks and not using our real names?"

"So, let's take the masks off and talk. You can ask me anything. Tell me anything. Say what you think needs to be said."

Leif sat back down. "What needs to be said? How about as soon as I mentioned money, your whole face changed. As soon as I said I was a broke college student, you shut down. I could see it. No, I'm not rolling in it. No, I didn't have to pay to get in. I couldn't afford it anyway. But I have integrity and pride, and that is something that money cannot buy."

"I don't care about the money," Rogue said quietly. "That's not what . . . it wasn't what you said about having no money that bothered me. It was . . ." He ran a hand over his face, obviously forgetting he had a mask on. Leif thought for a moment he was going to pull off his mask, but he didn't. "Sorry. If you want to go, I'll understand. I knew I shouldn't have come here tonight. I wasn't going to, but apparently anonymity isn't everything it's cracked up to be." He let go of Leif's hand and sagged back in his chair. "Fucking hate Christmas. I should have taken that vacation."

Leif stared at him, fairly certain he'd never seen a guy so defeated before. He looked utterly resigned and miserable. And Leif felt a bit stupid for having the antlers still on his head. "Which part of what I said upset you?"

Rogue's eyes met his. "I thought you were going to say something bad about this place, that's all."

What?

What an odd thing to say. And what the hell was wrong with Christmas?

"And why would that upset you?"

"Because I didn't want to hear it. I didn't want it to make things awkward, and then it got awkward anyway, so it doesn't matter. I'm sorry. I should go . . ."

Now it was Leif who took his hand and stopped him from leaving. "Rogue."

"My name's not Rogue," he said. Then he pulled off his mask and sat silent for a long second as though he was waiting for something. Then he tilted his head just so. "You don't know who I am?"

Leif shook his head. He was handsome, hot as hell. But Leif didn't recognize him. "Should I?"

Rogue, or not Rogue, apparently, stared for another beat, then he smiled. And then his smile grew bigger and he eventually laughed, shaking his head. And wow, what a stunning smile it was. "No. Not at all. You know what? If you're still up for it, let's get drunk, let's dance, and let's forget about real life for a while. And if you're not opposed, I'd really like to make out with you some more because, holy shit, you can kiss."

Leif laughed, because really, that sounded really fucking good.

CHAPTER SEVEN

HE HAS no idea who I am. I took the mask off, and he still doesn't know me.

Russ had never felt so relieved. He'd wanted a night of anonymity and now he could have it, even without the mask.

And while that was true with Rudolph, it certainly wasn't for the rest of the crowd. Russ was surprised he hadn't been spotted yet, and he'd even had the mask off for a few seconds. He would have to put it back on.

"I'm still up for it," he replied. "And I'm not even opposed to the making out because, honestly, I thought the one with the talent was you."

Russ grinned at him, pulled the mask back on and stood up. He felt different then, like he was free, he had nothing to lose. Rudolph had already seen his face, and there was no recognition in his eyes. So Russ could be himself, because Rudolph had no idea who that was.

Russ took his hand and led him back to the bar. He ordered more drinks, and when he handed Rudolph his vodka, Russ stood right up close and slid his hand into the back pocket of Rudolph's jeans. He leaned in close enough so Rudolph could hear him, his lips brushing against his ear. "The music is louder down near the bar so I have to stand really close if we want to have a conversation."

He grinned. "Is that right?" But he clearly didn't mind too much because he slid his arm around Russ's back.

Russ tried not to think about how nice it felt or how much he missed that simple contact. "So can I get your real name?" Russ asked. "I mean, I can keep calling you Rudolph if you want, but you're too sexy to be a Rudolph."

He laughed. "What if my name was actually Rudolph?"

"Then you would be the sexiest Rudolph, probably ever."

He was still smiling. "It's Leif. And no, not like the leaf on a tree. L-e-i-f."

Leif.

"Now *that* is a sexy name," Russ replied, then gently tugged on the leash and brought their lips together.

"God that's so fucking hot," a voice said beside them, and Leif smiled into the kiss. They stopped kissing but stayed pressed against each other. Their friends were beside them now; Caleb and the kitty cat were a little sweaty and they both had reddened lips. "We need a drink," kitty cat said. Smiling, he swished his leather braids and gently swatted Caleb. "This Santa's Elf is on the naughty list, I'm sure of it."

"If I'm not already, I will be by the end of the night," Caleb said and pushed kitty cat up against the bar, kissing him hard.

Leif laughed. "God. I thought Jamie was bad. He's met his match tonight."

"Is that his name?"

"Oh sorry, I kinda suck at secrecy. But yeah."

"That's fine. Just means I don't have to call him kitty cat in my head anymore."

"He'd probably prefer it if you did."

Russ met Leif's eyes. "Tell me, Leif, all about your industrial design."

"You want to hear about my art?"

"Yes. All of it. I've actually been looking at some designers with my work, and nothing I'm seeing is what I'm after. And you're clearly very good at what you do," he said, looking up at the antlers, but he had to lean back in close so Leif could hear him. "Everything is drab and pretentious. I want edge and style, but nothing is coming close. So tell me, what am I missing?"

He gave that a thought for a moment. "I don't think it's what you're missing. Maybe there's something in your brief that's missing. If everyone has missed the mark, I think you're not clear about what you're asking for or you're asking the wrong people."

Russ pulled back a little so he could look into Leif's clear blue eyes. "Maybe I am. Maybe I haven't asked the right person."

Leif stared, and they were so close their noses were almost touching. "You need to be clear with your vision. Know exactly what you want and ask for it."

Russ's eyes were drawn to his lips, then back to his eyes. This conversation had two meanings; Russ was sure of it. "And what if they think I'm too bossy or demanding?"

"Then you're asking the wrong people," Leif murmured before kissing him again. He palmed the back of Russ's head, and my God, Russ could just let himself give in so easily . . .

He wanted to.

He wanted to take Leif home and kiss and talk and kiss

some more, and fuck, and he wanted to know what made him tick, what made him come undone.

"Ask me," Leif whispered against his lips.

Russ's mind swirled. Had he said something out loud?

"Ask me," he repeated.

"Come home with me?" Russ had no clue if that's what Leif expected to hear, but it was what he wanted to say.

Leif smiled. "Okay." He was looking a little drunk and a little dreamy. "Oh, I came here with Jamie. He'll have no way home . . ."

Russ took Leif's hand and looked over to where Caleb and Jamie were now kissing and laughing. "We're leaving," Russ told Caleb. "I'll take a cab so you can have the car. Please make sure your little kitten gets home safely, okay?"

"Yes, of course," he answered delightedly.

"Even if it's lunchtime tomorrow, make sure he gets home," Russ pressed.

Caleb smiled and pulled Jamie's harness so they were flush, and Jamie nudged him and began to purr. "I won't let him out of my sight," Caleb said.

Russ turned to Leif. "I promise he'll be returned home as soon as he wants. Are you still happy to leave?"

Leif nodded. "Yeah." Then he took the leash handle from around his wrist and handed it to Russ. "If we're gonna do this properly . . ."

Russ's blood began to hum. Hell yes, they were doing this properly. Russ took the leash, his gaze intense, and he gave it a gentle tug. Leif pulled forward, their fronts almost touching, their faces just an inch apart. "I'm honored, and when I get you home . . ." Then Russ stopped. Leif was shirtless. It was freezing outside. "Do you have a coat? I can give you mine if you need . . ."

Leif fished into his jeans pocket and pulled out a ticket. "Coatroom."

Russ took the small slip of paper with his free hand and led Leif through the crowd by his leash.

People watched, people moved to create a path, and Russ couldn't help but like it. They had no clue who he was. Actually, Russ was mostly incidental. They were all looking at Leif. He truly was striking.

Russ handed over the coat ticket at the counter near the exit, and the clerk soon returned with an old peacoat. It was a bit military in a Sgt. *Pepper* kind of way and vintage-cool. Leif slipped it on and wrapped the front around him, and they stepped out into the cold night air.

The doorman held the door, and the guy standing with him looked twice at Russ. "Mr. Q?"

Russ liked that his driver recognized him even in disguise. "Michael, I won't be needing the car tonight, but please make sure Caleb and his friend get home safely. I can only apologize for anything they do or say in the back seat."

Michael laughed. "No problem, Mr. Q. You have a good night." Then he looked up at Leif and his antlers and only then seemed to notice Russ was holding a leash. "I can drive you real quick and be back to pick up Caleb, if you'd prefer..."

"No, it's fine," Russ said, walking toward the taxicab stand. "But thank you."

Russ held the door to the first cab open, and Leif had to take off the headpiece so he could climb in. Russ followed in after him and gave his address to the driver. He turned back to get a good look at Leif without the antlers. The antlers sat on his lap, and they took up a lot of room and looked a little macabre in the darkness. But Russ could see now that the headpiece and mask were all one piece.

Leif was scrubbing his fingers through his hair. Definitely blond, almost white-blond, and a little long but shaggy in an artsy kind of style. "Ugh, it feels good to take that headband off." And when he glanced at Russ, his face on full display, his smile faltered. "What? Disappointed?"

Leif had an unconventional beauty. Like a runway model or a Viking or something remarkable and immeasurable. "Disappointed I can't kiss you right now," Russ answered. "Disappointed we're not back at my house already." Russ couldn't stop staring at him. "You are extraordinarily beautiful."

Leif laughed as if embarrassed. "Why can't you kiss me right now?"

"Because you have an artful masquerade mask of stabbing implements in your lap."

Leif was still smiling, and he leaned his head back away from the antlers and angled toward Russ. "I'm game if you are."

Russ couldn't help himself, stabbing implements be damned. He leaned back away from the antlers and kissed Leif. It wasn't hot and heavy, there was no frantic stripping of clothes or fumbling with zippers. It was just soft and sweet, with a hint of tongue and a promise of what was to come.

"Ah, this is your stop," the cab driver said, interrupting them.

Russ looked out the window to see, yes, they'd already arrived. And yes, it was dark so Leif wouldn't see the outside of his house. Which was stupid because he was about to see the inside, but if he could put off revealing who he was for another few seconds, he would. Leif might not have known his face, but surely he'd know his name.

Russ handed the driver the fare and a hefty tip and took

the antlers so Leif could climb out of the car. He didn't seem to notice the surroundings too much, but Russ handed him back the antlers so he could punch in his security code. He didn't have a front door key. He had pin codes and sensor lighting and sensor security cameras.

He entered the code, the door opened, and the entry hall lit up automatically as he stepped inside. He held the door open and watched the disbelief on Leif's face as he came in.

"It won't bite," Russ said. He closed the door behind them and took Leif's hand in case he was tempted to turn and run. He wanted to take the leash but didn't want to remove Leif's choice. He stood close and looked up into those pale blue eyes. He didn't want to lose that warmth, that spark and simmering flame of desire they'd had in the club and in the cab. "I'd really like to kiss you again."

"I'd like that too," he murmured, and thankfully, his attention was drawn back to Russ.

Russ wanted to keep it that way, so he slowly fingered the leash, waiting for permission. Leif smiled and held the antlers at his side, which Russ took as a green light, so he tugged on the leash until their lips met. And in an instant, that spark was fanned and the fire between them roared back to life. Russ walked backward, pulling Leif with him, their mouths joined, tongues entwined. It was a little awkward and they were both smiling as they made it to the living room. Russ left the lights off and led him upstairs towards his bedroom. They fumbled and laughed as the antlers caught in the railings, and if the upstairs hall hadn't been so wide, the antlers might have taken out the drywall, or someone's eye. They made it to the master suite, huge enough for ten king-sized beds, fronted by a wall of glass which became a mirror with the right lighting.

"Lights, dim," Russ said, and the lights came on, barely lit, subtle. Enough to see where the bed was, enough to see the lines of Leif's face, all angles and wide pale planes. Russ took the antlers from Leif and sat them carefully on the closest dresser, then turned to admire Leif in this light.

He looked ethereal and when Russ undid Leif's coat and slid it off his shoulders and let it fall to the floor, it took his breath away. "You are so beautiful," he said, kissing Leif's shoulder, his collar bone. He nudged his nose up Leif's collar to the sharp angle of his jaw, the soft skin below his ear.

Leif shivered.

"Are you cold?"

Leif chuckled. "Uh, no." He leaned into Russ a little. "Quite the opposite."

So Russ kissed that spot, that perfect join where his jaw and ear met, then he sucked the lobe into his mouth. Leif's reaction was deep and throaty, and his hands quickly found Russ's jacket.

It had some secret zipper and an inside button, and Russ cursed Caleb for buying it as they struggled to get it undone. But Leif laughed, and between the two of them, they got it undone. Russ tossed it onto the floor and then went to take his mask off.

Leif's hand stopped him. "Leave it on."

Russ couldn't help but smile. "Am I that unattractive?" He had seen him without it, after all.

Leif laughed again. "God no. But it's not every night I have a guy with a masquerade mask suck my dick."

Russ's eyes went wide, his pulse quickened. "Is that what you think I'm going to do?"

Leif cupped his face and pulled him in for a hard kiss.

"Yes. You can go to your knees, right here, and suck me. Then—" He smiled. "—you can fuck me."

Russ's breath caught, but heat burned from his insides out. From his bones and his belly, so hot he thought he might catch fire. He was normally the one who took charge and gave direction in the bedroom. To have someone else assume charge was . . . hot.

"Keep the collar on then," he replied.

Leif smiled. "Sure. And when you're done fucking me, you can wear it when I fuck you."

Russ stopped. Christ, he was going to actually combust at this rate. He hadn't bottomed in years. Not that he didn't enjoy it, he just found handing over control difficult sometimes. "I um . . ."

"You don't have to if you don't want," Leif said, a hint of a smile playing at his lips.

"I want to," Russ's mouth said without his brain's permission.

Is that really what I want?

Yeah, it is.

Leif's brash smile pulled at one corner of his mouth and he undid the fly of his jeans, the sound loud in the silence. He began to stroke himself.

Fuck.

So Russ went to his knees.

Leif's cock was directly in proportion with his body. Long, well-defined, and beautiful. Russ stilled Leif's hand, halting his slow strokes, looked up at him and opened his mouth.

Leif guided his cock in and Russ took over. He began to suck and lick, sliding his lips up and down his slick shaft.

He tasted delicious.

Russ looked up every now and then, and Leif had his

head back, groaning with the pleasure of it. Ignoring his own erection, Russ hummed and pulled off, making Leif look down at him. So Russ tongued the underside, smiling up at him. "Oh fuck, yes," Leif ground out.

"Do you want to come like this or when I fuck you?" Russ asked, tonguing the slit.

"Both." His voice was tight, clipped. "God, both."

Russ took him back into his mouth, sucked him hard and deep, and Leif's cock swelled and throbbed. His long groan and short breaths clipped in time with Russ's tempo.

"I'm gonna come," he hissed.

So Russ took him in as far as he could, sucked hard, and swallowed around him. Leif's hands fisted Russ's hair and he moaned as he came. Russ drank it all, reveling in the satisfaction of bringing such a sexy man undone.

He held the back of Leif's thighs, and probably just as well, because with one last long moan, Leif swayed. "Fuck."

Russ laughed as he got to his feet, holding onto Leif who was spaced out and smiling, his dick protruding from his jeans, half-hard. And that goddamn collar around his neck . . .

So hot.

"Here, this way," Russ coaxed him, leading him to the bed.

Leif sat down, then fell back on the bed, arms splayed out with his feet still on the floor. Russ lifted one of Leif's feet and undid his laces and pulled off his boot and sock, then he did the other foot. Russ briefly wondered if Leif had passed out, but his quiet laughter filled the room. "Jeans too, please, kind sir," Leif mumbled.

So Russ pulled on Leif's jeans until they slid to the floor with his boots and socks. Leif was completely naked on his bed—save the collar and leash—and he just lay there with all the confidence in the world. One hand twirled the leash, his other hand squeezing and stroking his softened cock. His gaze went from Russ's eyes to the bulge in his jeans. "Round two. Ding, ding, ding."

Russ laughed and remembered his thigh holster. He pulled out a condom and some lube and threw them onto the bed beside Leif. "You come prepared," Leif said with an amused smirk.

"It was that naughty elf's idea. I must remember to thank him," Russ admitted, then he began to undo his jeans. He undressed slowly under the heated scrutiny of Leif, who was still stroking himself on the bed.

He was so fucking hot. And that wasn't something Russ would normally tell a random one-nighter. Hell, he'd probably struggle to say that to a boyfriend. He'd never been good at expressing emotions or sexual wants and needs. But he was still wearing that mask, and it gave him obscurity and a brazenness he wouldn't normally allow. So he let himself say it. "You're the hottest guy I've ever seen. You're so fucking sexy."

And it wasn't just Leif's looks or his body. It was his confidence. His self-assuredness and being so comfortable in his own skin that he felt he could ask for whatever he wanted, touch himself without shame.

Leif sat up, smiling. He pointedly looked up and down Russ's now-naked form and hummed. "I could say the same about you." Then he put his hands to his collar and Russ thought for a moment he was going to take it off, but he didn't. He slid it around his neck so the O-ring and the leash were at the back, at his nape. Still smiling, he sidled over onto his belly and raised his ass a little.

"Fuck," Russ whispered.

"That was the offer," Leif said. "But if you'd rather stand and stare . . ."

Russ shook his head and knelt on the bed. He rubbed and kissed every inch of gloriously pale bare skin he could reach, then spread Leif's ass and rimmed him. Leif almost crawled up the bed, gasping and moaning, but Russ pulled him by his hips back into place. He couldn've used the leash, but he wanted to save that . . . "You like my tongue in your ass."

"Mmm," he replied, fisting the duvet and squirming. "Stop teasing me."

Russ chuckled and rolled the condom down his cock first, then applied lube to himself and then to Leif.

He moaned and whimpered when Russ pressed a finger inside him, and he rocked back and forth when Russ added a second. Leif was eager and desperate, and Russ was too turned on to wait any longer.

He pulled Leif up onto his all-fours and positioned himself between his legs. He took the leash in his right hand, wound it tight around his fist, and pulled. Hard enough that Leif could feel it but not hard enough to cause concern. Russ wanted Leif to feel realms of pleasure. He wasn't into pain.

Keeping the leash taut, Russ pushed inside him.

He was mind-blowingly tight, and so hot, Russ wasn't sure if he could stand it. He felt so incredibly good, and Leif arched his back and whined, but he took it. He took every inch of Russ, and holy fucking shit, he took it well.

"Fuck," Russ groaned. Then he began to thrust, and the intensity of pleasure ramped up another notch. "Oh God."

Leif rolled his hips and arched his back, pulling on the leash. Russ held him tight though, then used his hold on the leash to thrust into him, harder and deeper. Leif grunted with each pounding and Russ thought for a horrifying second that he'd hurt him, but Leif began to jerk himself off.

Fuck. He's turned on by this.

"You like this," Russ rasped. "Does that feel good?"

"God, yes," Leif replied. He let out a moan that might have even sounded pained. "So good."

"Can you come again? Like this?"

He groaned again. "Yeah, just don't stop."

So Russ didn't. He drove into him harder and deeper, and Leif got louder and he kept jerking himself, but Russ couldn't hold out forever. He was too close, too turned on, and Leif was too damn hot.

"I'm gonna come," Russ ground out, and he let go of the leash so he could drive his orgasm home. He gripped Leif's hips and thrust again and again. He was so engorged and so hard. Leif let out a strangled cry, and Russ came so hard the room spun.

His world went dark and he lost all sound, the only thing he was aware of was filling the condom deep inside Leif. When he came back to his senses, his face was pressed into Leif's back, his hands still on his hips, his cock still buried inside him. And Leif was shuddering through his own release.

"Holy shit," Russ breathed.

Russ wanted to collapse on the bed, he wanted to pull Leif into his arms and hold him, maybe even fall asleep like that.

Wake up like that.

But that's not what this was.

He pulled out slowly, and Leif slumped to his side.

"I'll be right back." Russ ducked into his bathroom, discarded the condom, and when he returned with a warm, wet washcloth, Leif hadn't moved. He put a hand on his hip. "Are you okay?"

"I'm so fucking okay right now, I don't want to move," he mumbled.

Russ chuckled, relieved. He pulled off his face mask and tossed it aside, then cleaned up Leif and the bed where he'd come the second time. He tossed the washcloth in a hamper, then knelt beside Leif. "Here, let me take this for you," he whispered, very carefully and gently unclasping the leash. He couldn't see any obvious red marks. "Does your neck hurt, or do you have any trouble swallowing or breathing?"

Leif laughed, and when Russ met his gaze, he found Leif staring into his eyes. "It's not my neck you should be concerned about."

"Was I too rough?" Russ was horrified. "Are you sore?"

Leif's smile lingered warmly. "You were just rough enough, and I'm just sore enough."

"Can I get you anything?" Russ tried.

"A name."

"A what?"

"A name. More specifically, *your* name."

"Oh." Russ hesitated and tried to smile it off. "I'll just put this over here," he said distractedly, taking the collar and leash and putting them beside the antler headpiece on the dresser.

"It's only fair," Leif said, still lying unmoving on the bed. "I've seen your face, had your cock inside me. You know my name, and I fully intend to fuck you in the morning, so . . ."

Russ laughed. He was standing completely naked in full view of him. Yet giving away his identity was a different kind of exposure.

"The guy at the bar called you Mr. Q," Leif said. He rolled onto his back, stretching a little. "And you were surprised when I didn't recognize you. Not offended, but amused."

Russ walked back to the bed and sat down. Would this change anything? Would it ruin their night? Russ couldn't change who he was, he couldn't be anyone else, and he certainly would never lie to him.

"My name's Russ."

"Ross?"

"Russ. R-u-s-s."

Leif sat up, his blond hair sticking out at all angles, his eyes wide. "Like Russ Quarringt . . ." Russ could see the moment realization dawned. "Oh, holy shit."

Russ smiled ruefully. "Exactly like Russ Quarrington."

CHAPTER EIGHT

SWEET BABY JESUS IN A MANGER, he was Russ Quarrington.

The Russ Quarrington.

I've just had Russ Quarrington's dick in my ass.

The Russ Quarrington's dick.

And what good dick it was. Actually, there wasn't one part about this whole night that Leif had not liked. Russ was honest with him at the club. He'd even removed his mask, revealing his identity to Leif before things got sexual between them. Only Leif hadn't known his face.

But Russ was kind and courteous, an incredible lover, gentle and generous afterward.

"Do you have a problem with that?" Russ asked. "Now you know who I am?"

Christ. He looked so guarded, as though his defensive walls were back in place. Did he encounter this often? Did he never get the chance to be himself before people realized who he was? Man, that would have to suck.

"My only problem right now," Leif said, "is that we're

not under the covers. I'm getting cold and I'm tired, and my body's starting to hurt in all the right places."

Russ shot him a look. "Hurt? Did I hurt you?"

Leif reached out and squeezed his arm. "Not hurt. Sorry, wrong word. Ache. I'm beginning to ache in all the right places." Leif pulled at the bedding, trying to pull the sheets down enough so he could climb underneath them. Then it occurred to him. "Oh, is it okay if I sleep here? I don't know if that's what you normally do or whatever . . ."

Russ stared at him for a moment, as though he couldn't quite understand something. Then he shook it off. "Yeah, of course, it's fine." He stood up and pulled the covers right back, and Leif maneuvered himself into position.

He lay down, snuggling in and pulling up the covers but holding them open for Russ. "I don't care if I'm on your side of the bed. I'm too comfortable to move."

Russ slid into bed, and they pulled the covers up. "You're not on my side. Are you still cold?" he asked. "I can fix the temperature to whatever you're comfortable with."

Leif shifted over to Russ and wriggled in close, laying his head on his chest. Russ's arm went around his shoulder. "I'll warm up, I'm sure," he said.

Russ chuckled. "Uh, now you're kind of on my side."

Leif sighed. "I just took your dick in my ass, so I'm allowed. That's just how it is. I don't make the rules."

Russ laughed again and rubbed Leif's arm, tightening his hold on him. "Lights off," he murmured, and the room went dark.

"That's pretty fucking cool," Leif mumbled. He was struggling to keep his eyes open. He wasn't joking when he said he was tired. And this bed was the most comfortable bed he'd ever lain on. The right ratio of firm and soft, the sheets felt smooth and luxurious, not like the cheap and scratchy ones he had. And the warmth and strength of Russ's arm, the sound of his heart under Leif's ear . . .

And just like the pricey digitized lighting in Russ's house, like someone had snapped their fingers and said lights out, Leif was asleep. Though his dreams took him straight back to Evoque, back to the masquerade gala . . .

"Why is being a reindeer fitting? Because these are reindeer games, are they not?" Leif waved to the crowd, to the bar, the masks, the pretense. "An exclusive club for the elite and invited few, while those who aren't allowed in, because they don't meet the financial requisites, aren't allowed to play."

Russ's stunned, offended expression . . . and how he'd stopped Leif from leaving. "Wait! Don't go, please. Sit with me and talk. I want to hear what you have to say."

"About what?"

"About everything. Be honest with me. No one is ever honest with me and I need to hear it."

"You're asking for honesty when we're wearing masks and not using our real names?"

"So let's take the masks off and talk. You can ask me anything. Tell me anything. Say what you think needs to be said."

Leif's indignation. "What needs to be said? How about as soon as I mentioned money, your whole face changed. As soon as I said I was a broke college student, you shut down. I could see it. No, I'm not rolling in it. No, I didn't have to pay to get in. I couldn't afford it anyway. But I have integrity and pride, and that is something that money cannot buy."

"I don't care about the money," Russ had said quietly. "Fucking hate Christmas."

Russ's face, utterly resigned and miserable. Defeated.
What the hell was wrong with Christmas?
Exactly like Russ Quarrington.
Russ Quarrington. Holy shit.
Do you have a problem with that?

Leif woke with a start, and a strong hand on his arm kept him in place. It was warm and reassuring, and Leif became aware of his surroundings.

He was lying on his side in the world's most comfortable bed. He was toasty warm and currently being the big spoon to a very well-fitting little spoon. His arm was holding the little spoon in place, and it must have been Russ's reassuring touch when he'd startled.

Russ.

He was in bed with Russ Quarrington.

Words floated through his mind before dissipating like mist . . . *Exactly like Russ Quarrington. Do you have a problem with that?*

"Morning," Russ said, rubbing Leif's arm.

"Morning," Leif croaked. He spoke into Russ's shoulder. No, he had no problem with that at all.

"Sleep okay?"

"Like the dead." It was then he became aware of his morning wood pressed firmly against Russ's ass. He pulled his hips away but kept his arm around him. "Sorry about that," he murmured. "My body likes waking up like this, apparently."

Russ chuckled. "I was going to get up and make you coffee but didn't want to move. I rather like waking up like this too, apparently."

Neither one of them moved.

"So," Russ hedged. "I have a proposition for you."

"A proposition?" Leif repeated, and Russ held his arm tight so he couldn't move.

"Yes, a proposition." There was a smile in Russ's voice, so Leif went along with it.

"And that is?"

"I'd like to remind you that you have a promise to fulfill this morning," he added, his tone formal but laced with humor. "But my question is this. Do you wish to collar and fuck me before coffee or after?"

Leif barked out a laugh into the back of Russ's neck. "Such a dilemma." He was going to say staying in bed and fucking was his preferred option, but his stomach replied with a loud growl on his behalf.

Russ laughed. "Breakfast it is." He peeled himself away and sat up with his feet on the floor. "I don't know if I'm disappointed or not," he mused, casting a smile over his shoulder. "I mean, I was all for the collaring and fucking before breakfast, but after's fine too." He stood up and his half-hard dick, thick and uncut, made Leif's mouth water.

Damn.

He hadn't really appreciated the man's body last night.

"Or we could stay in bed," Leif whispered.

"We could," Russ answered smugly. "Or I could feed you breakfast in my kitchen, and you could spend the entire time thinking about how much you want to be inside me and all the things you'll do to make it good for me."

"Is that right?" Leif asked with a laugh.

"Yep. Then we could shower and get reacquainted, and my bathroom is really close to my bed." He waved his hand to a door on the far wall. "Which is terribly convenient."

Leif laughed and stretched out. The bed was huge, even for his tall frame, and extremely comfortable. "I wouldn't be opposed to getting back in this bed later. This mattress is incredible."

Russ, still naked, grinned as he walked into the bathroom first. Leif heard him pee, then the faucet turn on. He came out with a towel, drying his hands and dabbing his face, then disappeared through another door still without a stitch of clothing on.

Leif noticed the room then. It was huge. Like huuuu-uge. The entirety of his mother's house could probably fit in this room alone. There was a wall of tinted glass, the huge bed, a fancy looking Japanese-style dresser. His antlers sat atop it, and it made him smile.

Christ. What a night.

"Here you go," Russ said. Leif hadn't heard him come out of the walk-in closet. He was dressed now, wearing black sweats and a gray shirt, and he threw a black T-shirt and a pair of sweatpants onto the bed. "They'll probably be too short in the leg for you, but it might be more comfortable than wearing last night's jeans and your peacoat to breakfast."

"Oh, thanks," Leif replied.

"I'll make a start on breakfast. Come down when you're dressed. Down the stairs, through the living room, and to your right."

Jesus. Did he need a map? Just how big was this house?

"Thank you," he said again.

"How do you like your coffee?"

"Uh, cream. No sugar, thanks." Leif sat up; the blankets puddled at his waist. It was the middle of winter and he wasn't even cold. If he'd been at home, he'd have socks and a sweater on with his sweatpants.

"No rush," Russ said. "If you want to nap for another five or ten, that's fine too."

Leif scrubbed his hand over his face. "Nah, I should get up. What time is it?"

"Eight thirty." Then Russ frowned. "Do you have somewhere to be today? I didn't even ask, sorry. That was rude of me, I just . . ."

"You just what?"

"Oh, well, I just . . ." He ran his hand through his hair. "I just didn't think to ask."

"How long should I be expected to be here today? If you need me to leave, that's fine." Leif wasn't sure what he wanted that answer to be. He was intrigued by Russ. He was interested to see what made the enigma tick.

"You can stay as long as you want today. I have no immediate plans," Russ replied, which implied that Russ would have him here all day long? Or that he didn't care either way? It was hard to tell.

Leif didn't know him well enough to guess. But he was earnest and polite in his offer, so Leif decided to go with honesty with a dash of reality. "I have nowhere else to be today either. Though I will have to do the obligatory 'Yes, I'm still alive' check-in at some point."

Russ almost smiled. "Yeah, of course," he said before walking out.

Leif used the bathroom and freshened up the best he could, given it was someone else's bathroom. He didn't want Russ to think he was snooping, so he wasted no time getting dressed, then followed his directions downstairs.

And holy shit.

When he'd wondered how big the house was, he couldn't have imagined it.

It was sleek and modern, minimalist with well-designed lines and use of light. Some walls were dark, some light, all of them tall. There were art pieces in reds and golds, blues and silver, furniture pieces that looked hand-built and made to order. It was straight out of an episode of *Million Dollar Listing*.

He found the kitchen, which had white marble counter-tops, white gloss cabinets, and expensive appliances. Russ was there, barefoot and busy cutting up some fruit.

Russ smiled when he saw him, and he handed him a mug of coffee. "Morning," he said.

Such a simple word made Leif's heart thump. Such a simple gesture in these very complicated surroundings.

"Your house is amazing," Leif said. He wasn't being cheesy or trying to make small talk. He meant it. And he didn't want Russ to think he was buttering him up just because it was a mansion. Leif actually appreciated the design. "The use of lines and light is incredibly clever. The depth perception is amazing. And I've only seen three rooms."

Russ stared at him, then laughed. "Oh, you're an art design student. That's right. I thought you were pulling my leg."

Leif sipped his coffee. His very good coffee. Better than a specialty café coffee. "No, I mean it. I'm duly impressed. By the architecture and the interior design, and the coffee. It's perfect, thank you."

"You're welcome."

"Didn't you say last night you were having trouble finding a designer?" Leif asked.

"I did."

Leif looked around the huge, impeccable kitchen to the outside garden, which also looked perfectly manicured, even in winter. "Well, I'd be starting with the person who did this place because, damn . . ."

Russ smiled as he popped half a strawberry in his

mouth. He slid the plate of diced fruit toward Leif, silently offering it to him. "Well, I *did* start with them," he said.

"And?"

"The person who did this place was me."

Leif stared at him. "Okay, first of all, wow. And second of all, why hire someone else when you should be doing it?"

Russ opted for a slice of kiwifruit and shrugged as he chewed. "I don't know. A few reasons, I guess. Time, being the first. I don't really have the time to be dealing with that right now. I like to hire local people and get that outside influence, ya know? But I don't know . . ."

Leif was confused. How could Russ Quarrington be uncertain about anything? "You dunno what?"

"Well, I don't know if what I'm doing is good enough." He shrugged again, but this time there was a layer of uncertainty and self-doubt to his defensiveness.

"I get that time isn't a luxury everyone has a lot of. But clearly you have pretty good taste and a great sense of style and space." Leif picked some more fruit and took a small bite, aiming for casual. "I'm not sure why you doubt yourself."

Russ's gaze darted to his; then he looked away. Yes, Leif had definitely struck the right nerve. He sipped his coffee instead of replying.

"Seems to me you don't have any reason to doubt your own ability," Leif added. "But you can show me around the rest of your house if you'd like my honest opinion."

Russ tried not to smile and failed. "Sure." He nodded to Leif's mug. "Bring your coffee."

Leif smiled as he followed Russ, both barefoot and sipping their brew as they went. Two things became very clear. One, Russ's house was huge and beautiful, and two, if you ever wanted to see Russ relax and be himself and hear him talk at will and without a hint of self-doubt, simply ask him about design and art and structure.

There were several living areas, an office, spare bedrooms, a game room, a media room, an in-house gym with a heated lap pool—which explained his incredible body—and a wine cellar. But the flow of the house was more than ergonomic. It was thoughtful and had purpose. Every space was sympathetic to height and light, and every furniture piece was art. And the artwork . . . Leif had only seen such pieces in magazines and catalogs.

Leif talked about the light fixtures and the lines of walls and angles of shadows, perspective and how such minimalist design was the hardest to get right.

"And this is done to perfection," he said. "Russ, there isn't one thing that doesn't compliment the overall design. This isn't just some Beautiful Homes episode; it's also a how-to-incorporate-art-into-living episode." He let out a breath, shaking his head at the stunning beauty of it. But he was dying to know something. "What's your favorite thing?"

"My favorite?"

"Yeah, everyone has a favorite."

"I do, but it's . . ."

"I want to see it."

Russ's smile became a grin. "Back this way," he said, heading through to one of the living spaces. It was what he'd called his quiet room, which he read in, apparently. The light in the late afternoons was the best in the house. The room was rectangular, the walls were dark, and there was a long cabinet along one wall, one of those artsy-looking wave-shaped chairs in peacock blue that was probably worth a few thousand dollars. The wall of glass overlooked the northwest gardens, and it was a stunning view. Leif could imagine the light in here in the afternoons. But Russ didn't look at the view. He stood with his back to the cabinet and stared at the wall opposite. "This," he murmured, "is my favorite thing."

Leif stood beside him, leaned against the cabinet just like Russ, and looked at the wall. The ceilings were like twelve feet high, and this wall had a huge panel of what looked like rusted metal from floor to ceiling, maybe eight feet wide. The panels on either side were dark gray, but the panel of rusted metal was . . . well, it took Leif's breath away.

"Wow," he whispered.

Russ glanced sideways at him. "It's amazing, isn't it?"

Leif pushed off from the cabinet and put his hand to the rusted wall. "Is that . . . ?" He looked back at Russ. "What metal is that?"

"Iron pressed panel. Oxidized."

"It's absolutely beautiful," Leif said, running his hand over it, feeling the roughness, the coolness of it.

Russ stood beside him at the wall, grinning now. "It changes color with the light. In the morning, like now, it's kind of umber; and then it becomes more burnished as the afternoon goes on; then it almost looks red in the sunset." He seemed embarrassed, and he pulled his hand back from the wall and shook his head. "I played around with different kinds of metal and which aspects would play with which light—"

"You made this?" Leif couldn't hide his disbelief. Russ nodded and Leif threw up his hands. "Then you certainly don't need my opinion on anything. I consider myself schooled. Russ this is stunning."

He tilted his head. "You like it?"

That insecurity was back. "Love it. I can see why it's your favorite."

He let out a relieved breath, his smile genuine. "Which did you like the most?"

"Well, this wall is a masterpiece," Leif claimed. "But for me it's not one thing. I think the brilliance is in the sum of the parts. You manage to do bold and understated at the same time, and I'm very impressed."

Russ smiled in a way that made Leif's heart stutter. He got the feeling not many people got to see that smile. It was cute and shy, a little bit proud, and almost boyish. There was depth and warmth in Russ's eyes. He was unshaven, he had bed hair, and he was utterly gorgeous.

"You know what would look good against this wall?" Russ asked. "Your reindeer antlers. On some ornate, rustic stand or pillar. They would be a feature against this wall."

"Those antlers?" Leif repeated. "I don't know about that. They're hardly decent. I mean, for a masquerade party, sure. They were fun, and I'm sure the dark hid a lot of misgivings. But for a singular piece? Against this wall?" Surely freaking not.

"Now who's the one doubting his ability?"

"I could make you another set. With real wrought iron, authentic, and so much better."

"You could." Russ shrugged. "But they wouldn't be the ones you were wearing. When I first saw you wearing them . . ."

Leif nudged him with his elbow. "Have a thing for reindeer?"

"No." He met Leif's gaze. "I have a thing for confidence and audacity. For a guy who would dare. Who doesn't care what other people think. He who would make himself almost eight feet tall and command the attention of everyone there, but didn't care one bit for the attention."

Leif was stunned. Had he really read that much into it? Had Leif been so transparent with him?

Russ reached up and thumbed Leif's jaw, kicking Leif's pulse up a notch. Such an intimate touch . . . "He who was the sexiest man in the whole club, and he had no idea."

"I dunno," Leif said. "There was some *Assassin's Creed* guy who caught my eye."

Russ blushed and lowered his hand. His gaze darted to the wintery day outside. "And he had no idea who I was."

"Were you offended I didn't recognize you?"

"God no. Relieved. I wasn't going to go at all, but Caleb convinced me. He said I could have a night of anonymity and mystery, because when do I ever get to do that?"

"He was right."

His brow furrowed. "And now you know who I am . . ."

"And it doesn't change anything," Leif said. "For me, I mean. Hey, do you remember going to Ace's Wild the other day?"

Russ gave him a wary look. "Yeah."

"Well, apparently we just missed each other. I was talking to Ace and told him we were going to Evoque, and he said, 'Oh, that guy walking out is the owner.' I couldn't see your face at all. I didn't think much of it, to be honest. But Ace said you are kind and generous and down to earth. And well, he wasn't wrong."

Russ's brow creased. "Is that what he said?"

"Yep. Oh, and that you were quiet but very nice."

He stared out the window for a while, watching cold flurries swirl on the breeze, and Leif was certain he'd said the wrong thing. Russ seemed to be shutting down on him, and Leif was about to apologize, but Russ spoke. "It's not easy. Letting people in. I don't have a lot of people in my life. Which is as sad and depressing as it sounds, but I don't know who I can trust. Who likes me for me or who just wants my money . . ."

Leif reached over and took Russ's hand. "It can't be easy."

Russ's eyes met Leif's and he was still guarded, but there was a flicker of what looked like hope. "It's not. And I don't mean to sound like a poor little rich boy. I don't mean to sound ungrateful. It's just . . . I'm very isolated. And it's of my own doing. In the beginning it was what I wanted, but now . . . I dunno." His brow furrowed and he deflated a little. "Just feels like I'm a prisoner in my own castle, ya know?"

Leif squeezed his hand, but before he could speak, Russ pulled his hand free and ran it through his hair. "I'm sorry for unloading. I didn't mean to dump all that on you." And just like that, the wall was back up. The barrier in his eyes and smile was there, shielding the real Russ.

It was the last thing Leif wanted. He liked Russ. The real him, the part he didn't show anyone. Leif wanted Russ to feel free around him, not be wary and guarded. So, he navigated the conversation back to safer waters.

"You have nothing to apologize for. Well, maybe for not offering me another cup of coffee. Maybe some toast or something. And maybe you could pull out the plans you have for that place you need a designer for, and together we can brainstorm some ideas."

Russ frowned at the floor for a second, then he shot Leif a look and his lips curled with the beginning of a smile. "Yeah, okay."

"Oh, and I'll need to find my phone, and I probably should call Jamie and make sure he survived last night. And your friend Caleb," Leif added. "And we have that 'getting reacquainted in the shower' thing you mentioned, and of course the next round of sex."

Finally, Russ chuckled. "For a minute there, I was wondering where the bossy side of you went."

Leif preened victoriously at the return of Russ's smile. "Don't worry. My bossy side is never far away."

CHAPTER NINE

THE ONLY BREAD Russ had for toasting was the honey and sesame seed bagels he had on special order from the artisan bakery in town. He pulled out some fancy cream cheeses and a selection of berries and honeys, and Leif made a joke about how normal toast would have been perfectly fine, but he soon shut up when he tasted how delicious it was. And the coffee.

Russ would be lying if he didn't like the noises Leif made. The hums of appreciation, the moans as he enjoyed his breakfast. But what he liked the most was having company. Making breakfast for someone, laughing and talking over the kitchen countertop.

That's what he liked the most.

That's what he missed. What was missing from his life.

He couldn't ignore the pang of longing or the stab of loneliness that followed it. He knew he'd have to deal with it later, but for now, at least while Leif was still there, he'd let himself enjoy the moment.

Leif found his phone and sent his friend Jamie a quick text; then he talked with Russ about his schooling. He only had a year to go, and he wasn't sure what that meant for him professionally. He was reluctant to take a full-time factory job because he didn't want to give up on his art. He really liked his design teacher, even though he was sure she didn't quite understand his vision.

"What is your style exactly?" Russ asked. "Were the reindeer antlers true to your style or were they a leap in creative dissonance?"

"Those were me all over," he replied with a smile. "Here, let me show you." He took out his phone, stood in nice and close, opened some picture album, and began scrolling through photos before handing the phone to Russ. "Some of the photos aren't great. I'm no photographer and my phone's pretty old. But you can see the pieces. I take progressive shots. Beginning, middle, and end kind of thing. It helps me to see the stages."

There were so many different photos, different objects. Mostly statement pieces, but all incredibly conceptual and intellectual, very robust in design yet delicate in feature.

His art was sculpture, installation, 3D, and the reuse of objects. He used woods and metals, and each piece told a story. There were statues and furniture and hanging artworks. A chair, a cabinet, a table. A mirror and a chandelier. A statue of a charging bull made from twisted metal and nails.

"My style," Leif said quietly, "is probably modern-brutalist but abstract. I weld stuff and hammer out old copper plates and use wood and leather."

Russ turned to face Leif, looking him right in the eye. "Leif, these are incredible."

He smiled but shrugged the compliment off. "They're certainly not mainstream."

Russ set the phone on the counter and put his hand on Leif's arm. "No, I mean it. Leif, you have serious talent."

"Oh, thanks . . ."

"I want to show you something," Russ said. His excitement ratcheted up a notch. He dashed out of the kitchen, but when he realized Leif wasn't following, he stopped and waved him along. "I need you to come with me."

Leif laughed as he followed Russ back to his office. Russ slung himself into his desk chair, and a few seconds and some taps of the keyboard later, the screens were illuminated. He glanced up at Leif, just about to explain what he was doing, when he saw Leif was staring at a statue on the lowboy in the corner. Then Leif went over to it, and without taking his eyes off the statue, he stepped right and leaned out, then he looked back at Russ. His smile was huge. "That's awesome."

Russ shouldn't have been surprised Leif spotted it. "It is. If I had known your art style when I gave the house tour, I would've pointed it out."

Leif leaned in, inspecting it but not touching. The statue was roughly the size of a basketball and very much abstract and brutalist. Standing straight on, it appeared to be a deconstructed sculpture of a man's head, using blocks of blackened squares and rectangles of wood. It looked like Picasso had built his abstract portrait out of wooden blocks, then set the whole thing on fire. But if you looked at it from the left or right, as opposed to directly forward, the sculpture became a human heart. Still made of wooden blocks, then set on fire.

"It's called *serce czlowieka*," Russ said, getting up from his seat and walking over to him. "Which is Polish for the heart of man, or something like that. Remarkable, is it not?

That perception really does come from how you look at things."

"I love it," Leif said. His eyes were alight with wonder and a keen curiosity. "How did you come across it?"

"Auction," Russ answered. "It's a Kaminski."

Leif gawped and looked at Russ like he'd swallowed something too big for this throat. "Kaminski . . . ?" He took a small step back from it as though his mere presence might make it fall over.

Russ laughed. "Touch it," he said, picking it up. "It's kind of crazy. When I first saw it, I thought it was charcoal or something, and I expected to be covered in ash or soot, but it's not . . ."

Leif whispered. "Please don't touch the expensive art pieces."

Russ chuckled. "Is that your museum-curator whisper?"

Leif stared at him. "Yes. It's a Kaminski!" He put his hand to his forehead. "Christ."

Russ laughed now and set the piece back down. "From what I've seen of your art, I might even dare to say you're better than him."

Leif looked at him as though he'd just blasphemed the holiest of gods.

Russ probably shouldn't have found his expression so funny. He put a reassuring hand on his arm. "And you could even ask for the price tag to match."

He shook his head. "Yeah, no. Probably not. Ever. In this lifetime or the next."

Russ sat back at his desk and tapped on the keyboard again until he had the program he was after. "I'm not an art critic. I'm not a professional. But I know what I like, and I know excellence." Then he ever so casually threw Leif's words back at him. "So why do you doubt yourself?"

"I uh . . . I um . . ." He frowned at Russ, then turned back to the Kaminski piece. "Because I'm me. My workshop is my mom's old garage. I learned to use disregarded materials because I couldn't afford new supplies. The junkers and scrappers would keep odds and ends put aside for me when I was in high school. I guess they felt sorry for me. Most kids were playing football or getting high, and I'd be scavenging for parts."

Russ gave him his full attention. The kind of attention a statement like that deserved. "I think that makes your vision worth more. It comes from a place of integrity and drive. What is art when there's no passion behind it?"

Leif studied him for a long moment. Russ had no idea what he thought of that, but he assumed it struck a chord because Leif came around to his side of the desk. He parked his backside on the edge, close enough to be touching but not quite. "You seem to know a lot about art," Leif murmured. "I thought you were into real estate and development, or whatever."

Russ smiled. "I am into real estate, property development and private and commercial business enterprises, and whatever. But art is a love of mine. I never set out to like it, it just happened that way. But I choose what appeals to me. I certainly can't create it."

Leif sighed and eventually a smile won out. "What did you want to show me? Apart from the Kaminski. Oh God, do you have any other modern-brutalist god's art anywhere?"

"I have some other pieces you might like. But no more Kaminskis."

"Man. When you were showing me around earlier, I was so busy looking at lines and light, I didn't really look at your art. I actually thought your furniture was actual art. I didn't look at your *art* art."

Russ clicked a few more keys on his keyboard. "That's what I wanted to show you. You said you wanted to see the plans, but I have this 3D walk-through instead, and you mentioned lines and light . . ."

Leif studied the screen and watched as Russ took him on a virtual tour of the loft. The architecture was done, and it was basically a blank canvas. Russ just needed someone with the right vision.

Someone with edge and conviction in their craft.

And Leif talked about the brief, specifications, and finer points of execution, discussing the matter as if he were helping Russ find someone else.

But Russ was almost certain he'd found the guy he wanted.

"Purpose and function are the critical aspects though," Leif added. "What is this space for again? Did you tell me that last night? I can't remember."

"It's an executive living space," Russ answered.

"Is that realtor speak for a really fancy and expensive condo?"

Russ chuckled. "Yep. Basically."

"Who's it for? Is it for you, or are you selling it?"

"I don't know yet. I can't decide."

"Decide on what?"

Russ leaned back in his chair, looked up at Leif, and sighed. "Decide if I want to live there."

Leif's eyes went wide. "And leave the most beautiful house in the world?" Then he balked. "Oh, is this fancy condo not in Vintage Ridge? Is it like in London or something?"

Russ saw the flicker of disappointment in Leif's eyes,

and he dared dream for one brief and wonderful moment that disappointment was for him. That he was moving away or that he had a life somewhere else, and Leif was disappointed that any chance of another date wasn't likely. He wished it was for him, but how likely was that?

Leif had a whole life outside of their chance meeting. He had school, a family, close friends. It was Russ who had none of those things . . .

"No, it's for me," he answered eventually. "This house is beautiful, yes. And I love it. But it's too big for just me. I think I want something smaller, in the city. I'm undecided yet." A house had to be many things, but above all, it needed to be a home.

"I get that," Leif replied. "It is big. But it feels like a home. It's not cold and vast like you might assume because of its size. It's surprisingly warm and lovely."

Russ found himself smiling at him, because it was as though Leif had just read his mind. "Thank you." Then he had an idea . . . "I could take you to see it if you want. The loft, that is. You could tell me what you think. I'd be very interested in hearing your thoughts about interior design."

"Me?"

"Yes, you."

"Now, or after our shower and next round of amazing sex?"

Russ laughed. "I'm not sure if it'll be amazing." His face grew hot and he didn't dare wonder what color of red he was. "I mean, well, yeah . . . it's been a while since I . . . I haven't bottomed in a really long time, so . . ."

Leif, still leaning against the desk, reached down and took Russ's hand. "So I will take my time and make sure you enjoy every second."

Russ's blush deepened.

"You can wear my antlers if you want," Leif offered. "Or would you prefer I wear them and you can wear the collar?"

Russ was so overwhelmed with the casual talk of such things, not to mention the mental images now flaunting through his mind. "Damn . . ."

Leif laughed. "Shower first though, right? I feel kinda funky, and I could brush my teeth. If you have a spare toothbrush." He held up a finger. "I mean, I did bring one I can use if I *have* to . . ."

"I'm sure I have a new one somewhere," Russ replied.

"Now the big question for you," Leif said excitedly. "Do you want to come in the shower, in bed before sex, during, or afterward? Both? All? None?"

Russ was certain his face was about to melt off, and his heart was about to gallop right out of his chest. "Um, I, uh . . ."

"You asked me this question last night, so it's only fair I return the favor."

Russ laughed, embarrassed but getting turned on at the thought of what they were about to do. "Shower," he replied.

"Mmm." Leif licked his lips.

"And after."

He laughed and drew his bottom lip between his teeth. "Twice. A man after my own heart." He took a deep breath and groaned on the release. He stood up from the desk, and Russ couldn't help but notice the bulge in Leif's sweatpants. "Okay, we need to get upstairs and get naked now."

Russ felt warm all over and a little light-headed with anticipation. But he managed to get to his feet and lead Leif up to his room. Russ kept hold of his hand. He'd missed the luxury of such a simple act; he wasn't letting go of his hand until Leif pulled his away first.

When they stood in the bathroom, facing each other, Russ still didn't want to let go. Not of Leif's hand, not of this moment. Not of the connection between them that had little to do with the desire in Leif's eyes and more to do with the ache in Russ's chest.

And like Leif somehow knew, like he could read his mind, he stayed close and kept touching him. Gentle caresses and sweeping thumbs, soft kisses on naked skin.

Russ found a new toothbrush in the bathroom cabinet, and they stood side by side and brushed their teeth. Russ couldn't help but smile as he brushed.

"Wha?" Leif asked, his toothbrush sticking out of his smiling lips.

Russ shook his head. How could he admit to finding joy in doing such a mundane, domestic task? But damn, it'd be real nice to have someone to share this with every day. "Nothing," he mumbled, then rinsed his mouth. "You just look really cute. That's an ad for Colgate right there."

Leif laughed as he rinsed his mouth, and then he rinsed out the toothbrush and popped it into the holder alongside Russ's. "In case I need to use it again," he said.

It was ridiculous how happy that made him. "I wouldn't be opposed to there being a next time," he whispered.

Leif's gaze met his and the air between them sparked with electricity. He put his fingers under Russ's chin and tilted his face before claiming his mouth with a kiss. A hard, sensual, minty-fresh kiss. "I've wanted to do that all morning," Leif murmured when he broke the kiss.

Russ's head spun with the thrill of it. "Wow."

Clearly very pleased with himself, Leif pulled his shirt

over his head and nodded toward the shower control panel. "How does that work?"

Russ chuckled and walked into the shower room. It was a walk-in tiled cubicle with a built-in LED screen for temperature control and water pressure. "Do you like it hot?"

Leif grinned. "Scorching."

Christ. Russ was already aroused. And when Leif stripped out of his sweats, Russ could see he was too. Fuck, he was so beautiful. Russ set the controls and stepped out to finish getting undressed.

"This bathroom is amazing," Leif said. He was completely naked, and Russ could barely focus on anything but him. "My eyes are up here," Leif said, pointing to his face. He was smug, so that was probably a good thing. "And you're still incredibly overdressed."

Russ nodded, then shook his head, then wondered what he was supposed to be doing. Oh, right. Clothes. "I can't think straight when you're naked."

Leif laughed and walked into the shower. He stood under the hot water, his head tilted back, and he moaned. "Oh my God, this shower is heaven."

He stayed like that, his eyes closed, and Russ was transfixed. He couldn't take his eyes off him.

"You naked yet?" Leif asked, not opening his eyes.

Russ pulled off his shirt and tossed it, then quickly threw his pants down and kicked them off. He took a moment to drink in the sight of the gloriously naked and wet man in his shower.

Leif blinked the water out of his eyes and held his hand out. "Oh, did you need a towel?" Russ asked, reaching for one.

"No. Your hand," he replied.

Russ took his hand and Leif pulled him into the shower, pushed him up against the tiled wall and kissed him like his life depended on it.

He made good on his promise of bringing him undone in the shower. Then he took him to bed and made short work of him there too.

Russ thought it was what he wanted. He thought it'd be the best thing to happen to him in years. And in a lot of ways, it was.

But it was also scary as hell.

Not the bottoming part. Leif was a true gentleman and a considerate lover. Every touch, every kiss, every single thing. And that was what scared Russ the most.

He got him ready with careful hands, probing, pushing, prepping, and whispered praising. Russ melted under his touch, into his kiss. When Leif finally pressed inside him, when he buried his cock inside, Russ gasped with the intrusion. Stretched, full, and complete.

Russ had forgotten what true pleasure felt like. To be adored and desired so entirely. He took every inch of Leif, over and over, slow and sensual. Each thrust, every mutual push and pull, ebb and flow, had exposed Russ in ways he wasn't prepared for.

Every vulnerability, every insecurity was laid open. And as though Leif knew exactly what Russ needed most, he tended to the most vulnerable part of him.

They might have taken their masks off the night before, but this was the real unmasking. The true unveiling. There was no hiding anymore.

Leif held him tight and kissed his mouth, his jaw, his neck. He whispered sweet nothings, he groaned with pleasure and he held Russ's face, staring into his eyes when his orgasm took hold. It wasn't just sex and it wasn't fucking. Leif made love to him.

It meant something.

Maybe not to Leif, but it sure as hell meant something to Russ. This contact, this intimacy, brought every single thing missing in Russ's life to the surface. All the love he'd been denied was right there in his touch, in his kiss.

He'd been in such a sullen funk for weeks, with everything missing in his life playing havoc in his head and heart. And now this with Leif. This perfect lovemaking, this perfect joining of bodies, and the flummox of emotions it set free . . .

Russ wondered if it was something he'd ever recover from.

CHAPTER TEN

SEX WITH RUSS WAS INTENSE. Leif had had all kinds of sex: hot, boring, wild, and weird. But nothing was intense as it was with Russ.

Leif took it slow and careful, gentle and deep. He held Russ's hands, cradled his face, wrapped his arms around him, held him . . . It was a kind of lovemaking that he felt in his soul. And when they'd both had enough, instead of things getting a little awkward between them, Leif simply made Russ the little spoon, wrapped him up tight, and they dozed off.

It was crazy how comfortable it was. Not just Russ's bed, but how comfortable Leif was with him.

And when Leif woke up, not only was his arm still around him, but Russ was holding his hand, clutching it to his chest. And sound asleep.

He was a mystery, that was for sure. Known by his name, by his brand, his reputation as an astute and successful businessman preceded him. But the private man wasn't like that at all. He was incredibly smart but he was funny and sweet too. But there was even more to Russ than that. There was an underlying sadness or a disjointed distance that he'd put between him and the rest of the world. There was so much more to him than met the eye. In fact, Leif wondered if he'd even barely scratched the surface.

When Russ stirred, Leif held him tight and kissed the side of his head. "Where were you going to go on your vacation?" he asked quietly.

It took him a moment. He didn't turn around, his voice croaked with sleep. "What vacation?"

"Last night at the club. You said you should have gone on that vacation."

He sighed. "I wasn't sure. Somewhere, anywhere warm. The Caribbean probably. It was only talk though. When Caleb insisted I go to the masquerade gala, I threatened to take a vacation so I'd miss both the gala and Christmas."

Leif chuckled. "Well, I'm glad you didn't go."

Russ relaxed into his arms. "Me too."

"What's wrong with Christmas?" Leif softened the question with a kiss behind his ear.

He sighed deeply. "I'm not a fan."

He didn't elaborate, and Leif didn't want to push. He knew Christmas could be a terrible time of year for a lot of people. "I never used to be," Leif added. "As a kid, I'd never know where I was going to be, and it was never a big deal at any of the homes I was in."

Russ stilled, then turned and rolled over to face him. His eyes were cautiously curious. "At any of the homes?"

Leif nodded. "Yeah. I was in foster care until I was six. Went to a bunch of different homes. But I was a gangly-looking kid; skinny, lanky, weird eyes."

"Weird eyes?" Russ frowned. "You have beautiful eyes."

Leif smiled and kissed him softly. "My eyes are a fraction too far apart. I kinda grew into my skull as I got older, I guess, but as a kid I might have looked a bit weird."

"I had no idea you were in foster care. I'm sorry."

"Don't be sorry. I got put into a home with my mom when I was six, and I've never left. I have five foster brothers and sisters who are my real siblings, and she's my real mom, I don't care what anyone says. We might all have different colored skin and different colored hair, but we're family."

Russ smiled, but there was a sadness lurking. "You have five brothers and sisters?"

He nodded cheerfully. "Yep. We never had much, but we had each other and we had Mom. And that was all we'd ever need. Christmas was never really about gifts. More about food and family. Though I started making Mom gifts from the very first Christmas. I spent the first Christmases I can remember in different homes, but no one wanted a gangly kid who drew pictures and made stuff with whatever paper or twigs he could find. They wanted a kid to play ball with."

Russ put his hand to Leif's face. "Sounds like you went with the right family in the end."

"I did." Leif kissed him again. "Tell me about your family?"

And just like that, a wall went up and his whole face changed. Gone was the kindness and openness, and in its place was a closed-off vacancy. "I don't have family."

Russ tried to look away, but Leif put his hand to his face, held his gaze, and thumbed his cheekbone. "I'm sorry to hear that."

"Me too."

"Family can be tough."

Russ frowned and closed his eyes. Maybe he didn't want Leif to see the truth in them. "Yeah."

Leif pulled him in, wrapped his arms around him, and kissed the side of his head. "You don't have to tell me what happened, but I'll listen if you need."

Russ didn't reply to that, but he made no attempt to leave Leif's embrace. If anything, he snuggled in a little closer. So Leif held him tighter and rubbed his back, and he thought for a moment that Russ might open up. But he didn't.

Lying there was nice. Leif had never really been a snuggler after sex, but it felt right with Russ. Well, his amazing bed felt right, but the man in his arms did too. The wind howled outside, but inside the house was toasty and warm. Everything was temperature controlled, apparently. Everything was on voice control too, which was incredibly cool, but Leif could easily forget it was winter.

Leif wasn't joking when he said Russ's house felt like a home. It did. Some huge open spaces could sometimes feel like a museum, but this house didn't. Though he could understand why Russ might have wanted to move into something smaller, Leif got the impression it wasn't the size of the house that bothered him too much . . .

Leif's phone rang from a pocket of sweatpants somewhere on the bathroom floor. He groaned. "That'll be Jamie."

"Did you want to take his call?"

"Not right now."

Russ chuckled into his neck but then pulled back, his eyes unreadable. "Will you tell him who you spent the night with?"

Now it was Leif's turn to frown. "Did you not want me to? I've never lied to him."

Russ chewed on his bottom lip. "I don't mind. I don't want you to lie. But I also don't want to read about it in the gossip pages of the Ridge Express. I've had that happen before . . . It wasn't fun."

Leif's first reaction was to be pissed that Russ would think that, but he quickly realized that Russ led a very different life than him. Gossip pages were a reality for him, and Russ was being honest with him. The least Leif could do was return the same. "That must have been really shitty. I'm sorry that happened to you. But I wouldn't do that. And Jamie wouldn't either."

"I didn't think you would, I just . . ."

Leif waited.

"I just hoped," Russ whispered, "that you wouldn't. But some guys just want their fifteen minutes."

"You make it last way longer than fifteen minutes," Leif joked.

"I meant fame, not sex." Russ laughed.

Leif ran his hand through Russ's hair, then cupped his jaw. He was happy to see him smiling again. He looked him right in the eye. "I won't tell anyone. You have my word." He was about to suggest maybe they could have a second date, or an official first date, when his phone rang again. "Ugh."

Russ laughed. "You better get that. How about we get dressed and I can show you the loft? It's downtown. So we could grab some lunch before I drive you home. If you want . . . If you'd rather just go home, I can take you right there."

Leif kissed him, smiling. "Lunch sounds good. And I'd like to see the loft, and you can tell me all about what design ideas you have."

Russ's smile was genuine and pure. "I'd really like that

too. I'll just grab a shower real quick because I'm covered in lube. You better call your friend before he files a missing person's report."

Russ peeled himself out of Leif's arms and rolled out of bed, and a second later, the shower started.

Leif smiled at the ceiling before he followed him in. Not into the shower, but to collect his phone. The missed calls were from Jamie, of course, so Leif shot him a quick text.

> All is well. Great night. Heading home soon.
> How was your night? Home yet?

The text bubble appeared to show he was replying.

> My night was great.
> Home now.
> Will tell u all about it.
> Think I know who your masked man was.
> Caleb-cat wouldn't tell me, but I can
> guess.

> Caleb-cat?

> LOL yes. He worked my kitty real good.

"Oh God," Leif replied out loud, scrunching his nose.

"Wassup?" Russ asked from the doorway, glistening wet with a white towel around his waist. "Everything okay?"

"Oh yeah. Jamie just has a way with words, that's all. He had a good night apparently, and your friend Caleb-cat didn't tell him who I left with."

Russ let the towel fall away and pulled on some underwear. "Caleb's a good guy. He understands me. Well, he understands why privacy's important."

"Do people really try and leech on to you?"

Russ stopped buttoning his jeans and stared. "Uh, yes. Unfortunately."

Leif grimaced. "That's awful."

Russ began to smile. "Did you want to get dressed, or would you like to stay sitting naked on the bed all day?" He raked his eyes down Leif's body. "Not that I'd complain . . ."

"Oh, right." Leif stood, very naked, and found his jeans from the night before. "I might need to borrow your shirt, the one I was wearing earlier, if that's okay? I didn't really dress last night as though I was expecting a sleepover somewhere."

"Of course it's okay. Will you be warm enough? I have a whole closet you can choose from. Help yourself."

"Nah, this'll be fine." He retrieved the shirt from the bathroom floor. He threw the sweatpants into the hamper. "I have my coat."

He finished getting dressed, and when his boots were tied, he found his coat and stopped at the reindeer antlers. He smiled as he touched one of the leaves on the headband. The gnarled black horns struck quite the silhouette on the pale wall behind them.

"The contrast is great, right?" Russ said beside him. He was wearing dark blue jeans and a navy sweater that Leif could tell was expensive by the type of knit. It was casual, but he looked a million dollars. "I think they'd make a statement in any room. A blank wall and these on a tall stand. Or even right where they are."

"I can make you a better pair. It won't take long. I'll just need to find the right materials, but they'll be bigger and even better. But you can have these too," Leif said quietly. "I like the idea of you having them."

Russ shot him a look. "You do?"

Leif nodded, looking back to the antlers. "Yep."

"Then I'll keep them in here," he replied. "In my private room, just for me. And every time I see them, I'll remember you." He laughed and shook his head. "I'll never forget when you walked into the club. Christ, that was an entrance. You're bound to have set the Vintage Ridge rumor mill on fire. Every man there wanted you, and no doubt everyone will want to know who you are."

Leif chuckled and waved that notion off. "Ugh. Let them guess. I don't care. No one will have a clue anyway. I'm far removed from those social circles."

Russ's smile turned rueful. "You're not missing much. Most of them aren't worth knowing." He sighed. "Come on, let's find some food. I'm starving."

RUSS'S CAR was a black two-door Maserati, and Leif had always doubted a car's ability to *purr*, but this car literally did. It was deep and smooth and luxurious, and Russ looked sexy as hell driving it.

But it was a recognizable car. People stared as they drove by, and not that they could see with the dark tinting, but Leif began to understand Russ's plight of being under constant public scrutiny.

"Have you considered getting a car that doesn't announce who you are?" Leif asked.

Russ shot him a look. "You don't like it?"

"Are you kidding? It's the sexiest car ever. But you said

you didn't much care for how everyone stared. You drive this, and they're going to stare."

Russ smirked. "If you could be miserable in an old Corolla or be miserable in a Maserati, which would you choose?"

Leif laughed. "I see your point." Though Russ's comment about being miserable caught him off guard. "Are you miserable, Russ?" he asked.

He made a face. "I didn't mean to say it like that."

But he didn't deny it.

He pulled into a parking lot and nodded toward a diner. "These guys do a killer chicken sandwich. Sound okay?"

Not what Leif was expecting Russ to choose, but yeah, whatever. "Sounds great."

"You look surprised," Russ said quietly.

"I am," Leif replied. "I thought you'd prefer something fancy or something . . . I don't know. This place looks like somewhere Jamie and I would go."

Russ flinched, and he tried to smile but couldn't quite get it right. "I'm just a normal guy."

"Hey." Leif snatched up Russ's hand. "I didn't mean anything by that. Not in a bad way. I actually think it's pretty cool that you're just a normal guy. I like that. And I'm sorry if what I said came out wrong."

He shrugged it off. "It's okay, honestly."

He might have said that, but it sure didn't feel like it was okay.

But they went inside the diner, and if Leif thought for one second that Russ brought him here to give the impression he could slum it with the 'normal guys,' Leif was wrong. The guy behind the counter brightened as soon as he saw him. "Ah, Mr. Russ," he said warmly. "So good to see you today. Can I get you your usual?"

His usual. So he came here a lot.

Russ held up two fingers. "Two, please."

They took a booth toward the back, and Leif couldn't help but smile. "You come here often?"

Russ nodded slowly and played with the condiment holder on the table. "I do. Food's good, service is great, and no one knows—or cares—who I am."

Leif could appreciate that.

Russ's eyebrows pinched and he licked his lips. He looked out the window, clearly trying to weigh up if he should say whatever it was he wanted to say.

"And?" Leif prompted gently.

"And it reminds me of my childhood," he answered quietly. "I used to hang out in a place just like this in Raleigh. That's where I'm from. I um . . ." He swallowed hard. "I'd hang out with my friends, or sometimes my mom and I would have dinner there if my dad was working late."

Wow, some pieces of the Russ Quarrington puzzle began to take shape. He chewed on his lip and studied the ketchup bottle, so Leif tapped his boot against Russ's to get his attention. He looked up, and Leif smiled. "Thank you."

"What for?"

"For sharing that with me."

Their lunch arrived, and Russ literally sagged with relief. He quickly changed the subject, bringing the conversation back to Leif and his art major and different designers. He was still so undecided about the loft space, but he was right about the sandwich. Leif washed it down with his soda. "That was amazing," he said, patting his belly for effect. "This whole place is amazing."

Russ laughed. "Told you. I'll take this over that five-star dining nonsense, any day." Then he reconsidered that. "Okay, well, I've had some incredible five-star meals as well, but if I wanted to impress someone, I wouldn't take them somewhere five-star. I'd bring them here."

Leif grinned. "Were you? Trying to impress me?"

His cheeks tinted pink. *Holy shit, he was trying to impress me.*

"I'd like to think I'd know someone's intentions if I brought them here. If they thought it was stupid or lame, I'd know we were never really gonna hit it off. If all they wanted was some wallet to pay for exclusive table reservations, I'm not interested."

"So this was a test?" Leif grinned as he sipped his Coke.

Russ tilted his head, just so, and shrugged. "Maybe?"

"Did I pass?"

His lips twisted upward; his eyes danced with light. "Maybe."

Just then, his phone buzzed again—it buzzed a lot—and he groaned at the message on the screen. It was from Caleb.

Answer my damn call.

"I need to call him back, I'm sorry. I've been ignoring his calls."

"It's fine. I'll go find the bathroom," Leif said, giving him some privacy.

When Leif came back out, he found Russ frowning at his phone. "Everything okay?"

"Oh, yeah," he replied. "Not really."

Well, shit. Leif sat back across from him, concerned, and took his hand. "What's up?"

"I have to go into the office," he said flatly. "There's an issue with one of my contractors on the Quarry Estate, and they've just realized they don't have the proper permit for work that's supposed to start at seven o'clock tomorrow morning. One sub-clause has been omitted."

"Oh." Leif frowned. "Yeah, that doesn't sound good."

Russ shot him a look with a flicker of confusion. Then he smiled. "No, I don't care about that. I mean, I do care. Obviously. If they missed it, then we missed it too, and it's a bit of a fuckup, but we deal with shit like that all the time."

Now it was Leif who was confused. "So, what's the problem?"

"I wanted to show you the loft." He shrugged, then chewed on the inside of his lip while frowning at his phone. "I was looking forward to that. I mean to say, I was looking forward to your opinion and seeing what you thought. But now I can't. I mean, Caleb could deal with it if it was an emergency, and he'll no doubt already have the planning execs on the way, but I should be there. We'll need to sign off on emergency works—"

"I could look another day," Leif said. Russ was flustered and rambling, which was cute, but Leif wasn't ready for this to be over just yet either. "Like Tuesday or Wednesday? If you have time. Or next weekend? I know you're busy."

Russ sighed as he smiled. "Really?"

"Really what?"

"You'd come and take a look at it with me?"

Leif met his gaze. "For sure. But I think we should make a date out of it. It will have to be dinner because I have class during the day, and no doubt you're busy as hell." Russ wore an odd expression, so Leif gave him an out. "Unless I'm reading this all wrong. I can take a look at your loft and give you my opinion if you want. No date necessary."

Russ startled, a mix of surprise, horrified and embarrassed. "No, a date is fine," Russ said quickly, flustered and blushing. "And dinner on Tuesday is great actually.

Tuesday or Wednesday, whichever suits you. I'd really like that. I wanted to see you again but didn't know how to ask." He laughed and shook his head. "Christ, I suck at this."

Leif smiled and reached over to give his hand a squeeze. "You can start by saying 'Leif, I had an amazing weekend with you, and I'd love to see you again. Please stay Tuesday night after our pizza and movie date so we can have more amazing sex.'"

Russ's cheeks brightened, but he wore that genuine smile Leif was certain he didn't show many people. "Pizza and a movie?"

"Yeah. Is that okay?"

Russ laughed, as though he'd become a little emotional and tried to shake it off. "Perfect. So perfect."

LEIF HAD BEEN in his workshop for all of one minute before Jamie let himself in. He was grinning from ear to ear. "You bagged Russ fucking Quarrington. Tell me I'm wrong. Tell me that wasn't his million-dollar car that just dropped you off." His grin somehow got wider. "Tell me I'm wrong!"

"The car's not worth a million dollars."

He scoffed. "To you and me it may as well be."

Leif couldn't argue that. "I'm not admitting to anything."

Jamie laughed like it was all a crazy game. "I knew something was up. Caleb said he worked for him; then your masked man tells him to take the car. I mean, who has a car with a driver? No one that we fucking know, I can tell you that much. Then we get in the car and the driver calls his boss Mr. Q. So I knew it was him." Still grinning, he shook his head. "I told you those reindeer antlers were a magnet."

He looked around the workshop. "Where are they? The antlers?"

"I left them at his house . . ."

"Aha! So you don't deny it. I saw his car, Leif. Just now when he dropped you off. Well, I assumed it was his car. And you spent all this time together? Just how good was the sex?"

Leif laughed and leaned against the wooden workbench. He knew Jamie would never let this go, and actually, it would only get worse the longer he fought it. "You can't say anything. You can't tell anyone."

Jamie almost jumped up and down. "Oh, holy shit, it was him, wasn't it?"

Leif nodded, trying not to smile too hard. "I didn't know it was him. Even after he took his mask off, I still didn't recognize him."

Jamie laughed, delighted. "Oh, I bet that impressed him."

"I think so, actually," he admitted. "Jamie, he's not like I expected at all. He's sooooo smart and he's just a really decent guy. He's down to earth and good in bed, like wow—"

"Holy shit."

"What?"

"You like him!"

Leif shrugged, aiming for noncommittal, but Jamie knew him too well. "I think I could, yeah. But it's a bit early for that, dontcha think?"

"Jesus fucking Christ and Mary, Peter, and Paul." Jamie put his hand to his forehead.

"Jamie, you can't tell anyone. Those trashy rags will do anything for a headline, and I promised him I wouldn't tell anyone. If he thinks I've betrayed him . . ."

"I won't tell anyone," he replied. "Who'd believe me anyway?"

Leif smiled and shook his head. The whole thing was crazy. "He's not at all what you'd expect. He loves art, and he has a Kaminski! A fucking Kaminski. Do you know how cool that is to me?"

"I don't know who or what that is or why it's cool. But because you're all aquiver, I'm assuming it's artsy."

Leif chuckled. "Yeah. Artsy and spectacular."

Jamie let out a long sigh, though he was still smiling. "Well shit, hey. And I suppose he's gorgeous and he's funny and has a nine-inch dick, because what else does a gazillion-aire need?"

Leif didn't laugh at that. "He is all those things, but you know what Russ Quarrington is besides rich and sexy and funny and a decent guy?"

"What's that?"

Leif shrugged. "He's lonely. He tries not to let it show, but I think it burns him from the inside out. He can have all the money in the world, but I really do think the guy is just . . . lonely."

CHAPTER ELEVEN

RUSS WAS VERY WELL aware that Caleb was eyeing him strangely. All through the meeting with the town planners and contractors, he could feel his eyes on him. Russ had managed to avoid the conversation he knew was coming, but the next morning, he *knew* it was coming.

The fact he'd made it till ten was a miracle.

Caleb came in holding two fresh cups of coffee. He put one in front of Russ, then sat opposite him, waiting expectantly.

"Thank you for organizing the meeting yesterday," Russ began. "On a Sunday too, so I really do appreciate that."

"It was no problem," he said easily. He crossed his legs and his gaze grew rather pointed. "Are you deliberately holding out on me about what happened after the masquerade gala? Because I haven't seen you this happy in a long time."

"And thanks for the coffee," Russ added, dragging out Caleb's misery. "I really appreciate it."

"I will cancel every meeting and every appointment

from here until eternity if you don't tell me what happened with Rudolph."

Russ laughed. "Rudolph . . . had a very shiny nose. All the other reindeer loved him."

"The fact you even have a sense of humor after the last few weeks of moping misery tells me Rudolph did indeed guide your sleigh that night." He sniffed. "You left with him Saturday night, and I interrupted something Sunday lunchtime, and you haven't stopped smiling yet. So spill."

"Moping misery?"

He sipped his coffee with a look that dared Russ to argue.

"Okay, okay. He was a great guy," Russ offered up after it was very clear Caleb wasn't there to play. "He's artistic and talented, and he's funny and caring, and I think maybe he's like no one I've ever met."

Caleb blinked, and his mouth opened, then shut, and opened again. "That is . . . not what I expected."

"What were you expecting?"

"For you to say the sex was great, or mediocre at best, or something. Or that he had some weird reindeer fetish. I don't know. Not that you *like* the guy."

Russ snorted. "There was no reindeer fetish." Though the collar and leash were fun. "I'm not telling you anything about the sex: great, mediocre or otherwise."

"You don't have to," Caleb deadpanned. "The fact you can't even speak without grinning tells me all I need to know."

Russ hid his smile behind his coffee. "And your night? You were friendly with Jamie?"

Caleb raised one eyebrow. "You know his name?"

"Yes, Leif told me. And I trust that you got him home okay?"

"Let's put it this way . . . if I was his Uber, it'd be a five-star rating."

Russ laughed again. "I'm glad to hear that."

"He was a lot of fun."

"Are you seeing him again?"

"We discussed possible future hookups. We linked up on Grindr." Russ took it that was the new equivalent of getting someone's number. Caleb cocked his head. "Wait . . . are you seeing your guy again?"

Russ's smile was probably answer enough, but he was just about giddy with the thought of it. He had to say something. "We have a date tomorrow night."

Caleb stared for a long moment. Then he stared out the window, across the city of Vintage Ridge. "Well, shit," he mumbled. "Should we organize flowers or reservations somewhere? Where were you thinking? Spinarelli's would be nice. I can make some calls. What's his favorite wine? Actually, if you give me his full name, I can do a social media check and I can—"

"Whoa, stop," Russ said, palm raised. "He doesn't want any five-star restaurant. Actually, we're going to have a pizza and movie night at my place."

Caleb almost choked on his coffee. "Was that his suggestion? Or yours? Because you do realize that *Netflix and chill* means something else, right?"

Russ chuckled. "I'm aware. But please don't search him out on social media. I know all I need to know." He didn't want Caleb finding out where Leif lived or that he was a student who lived with his foster mom to help her with bills and yard work. He'd assume that Leif was some kind of gold digger when Russ knew Leif wasn't like that. "Oh, and I think I've found the designer I'm after too. I'm showing Leif the loft on Tuesday. I've seen some photos of his work, and I think I might've found exactly what I've been looking for."

Caleb's lip pulled down in a wary smile. "I'm beginning to think you might have." He studied Russ for a moment. "A date, huh?"

Russ tried not to grin like an idiot. "Yes. I know, a rarity for me. I'm um . . ." He cleared his throat. "I'm trying not to get ahead of myself."

Caleb thankfully didn't say *it's too late for that* and shot him a determined look instead. "So we need to make sure you're prepared. What will you wear? Have you considered your pizza options? Maybe we should pre-book. I can do that for you today. I'll source some menus. Do you like woodfired?"

"I think I can manage—"

"Condoms and lubrication and PrEP is a given these days. Do you need—"

"Caleb! Stop. Please." Russ didn't know whether to laugh or scream. "It's fine. I can manage."

"At least let me make a list of movies to suggest. You want him to know you're creative and intelligent. The wrong movie choice could be bad. I'd suggest something from the World Movies selection. Or even a classic. Something that says romance, intrigue, but witty as well. I'll need to narrow the search."

Russ sighed. "I think I'm capable of suggesting a few movies."

"Or a TV series. Like *Game of Thrones* could be a worthy contender. And it could give you a window for future dates. You know, to watch more episodes." Caleb gave a nod, as though confirming stuff in his head. "I'll need to study TV shows as well."

Russ considered putting his foot down, but if it kept Caleb busy and put an end to this conversation, Russ was all for it. Not that it really mattered. Russ was pretty sure Caleb was going to do it anyway. "Thank you. That'd be great."

"Should I order some floral arrangem—"

"No."

"But—"

"No."

He opened his mouth and Russ raised his hand. "Stop." Caleb deflated like a kid who was just told he couldn't have sweets. "I appreciate the concern, but I have it covered. I want him to know—and like, hopefully—the real me. And perhaps we could not read so much into this date, okay? I'm trying not to get my hopes up, and your excitement isn't helping."

Seemingly appeased, he sighed with his usual flair. "Fine."

Now if only Russ could convince himself not to get his hopes up.

Only thirty-three hours to go.

EXCEPT HE DIDN'T HAVE to wait the full thirty-three hours. Russ had sent Leif a text at lunchtime. He'd been antsy and useless all damn day and had to make himself wait until noon before texting.

Just checking you're still good for tonight?

His reply came through immediately.

Sure. Unless . . .

Russ's heart almost stopped. *Unless what?*

Unless you want to make it earlier? I was going
to call around to the scrapyard at around
three. Wanna come with?

To a scrapyard?

Yep. I need art supplies.

Hell yes I wanna come with. I'll pick you up just
before three.

He checked his watch. Three hours was so much better than five.

Dress for the occasion ;)

Russ grinned at his phone. There was no way in hell he was telling Caleb he was heading to a junkyard as part of his date night. He'd probably call for an emergency tetanus shot.

Looking forward to it

Russ had never sent a smiley face in a text message in his life . . .

Christ.

"Take a fucking breath," he mumbled to himself. His thoughts were so scattered, he couldn't get his mind into gear today at all. He had emails to answer, reports to read, spreadsheets to go over, and stock market analysis to scrutinize. But every single thought he had kept going back to Leif.

"This is ridiculous," he mumbled. But then he stood and pulled on his coat. Fuck it. He snatched up his keys and phone and met Caleb on the way out. He had his arms full of files and rolled-up blueprints and was clearly surprised to see him. "I'm finishing up for the day. Everything can wait until tomorrow."

"What . . . ?" Caleb asked, stunned. Then his eyes went wide. "No, wait. One second." He ran to his desk, dumped everything, and came back holding a single sheet of paper. "Your movie selection. Categorized by genre, message, and in order of preference, of course. Depending on what message you're trying to send him, I'd start with the first—"

Russ took the list. "Thank you. See you tomorrow."

"Okay, good luck!" he said as Russ got to the elevator door. "Have fun. Oh, and if it's a disaster and you need me to call with a fake emergency, text me SOS and I'll get you out of there."

Russ laughed as he stepped into the elevator and he was still smiling as he drove out of the parking garage. It was absurd how excited he was. Man, how long had it been since he'd taken an afternoon off to do something fun?

Never.

He stopped at the bakery and bought some of those bagels Leif had liked, then across to the markets for some more fresh fruit, and on his way out, he spied a row of Christmas decorations. He'd never really indulged in any before or given them a second thought.

But right there, like it was a sign, was a bobblehead reindeer with antlers so big they were disproportionately funny. It made Russ smile, so of course he bought it.

Maybe Leif would think it was stupid . . .

If he did, then maybe Russ would just keep it as a reminder.

He smiled every time he saw Leif's masquerade antlers still perched up in his bedroom. They were the last thing he saw when he went to sleep and the first thing he saw when he woke up.

Christ. He was reading way too much into this.

Russ went home and cleaned—not that anything needed cleaning—changed the sheets on his bed, and finally, when he'd checked the time a hundred times in as many minutes, he had to stop himself from leaving too early.

This shit was getting ridiculous.

Changing into some jeans and a sweater, he pulled on his boots and coat, grabbed his scarf and gloves and made his way to Leif's place. It wasn't a part of town he'd been to often, and the row of houses in Leif's street was old and faded, but given the street backed onto woodlands, Russ thought it would look pretty in fall.

When he pulled up, Leif was throwing something into the back of an old blue pickup. He saw Russ's car and grinned, and that immediate response made him feel giddy. Russ tried not to smile too hard when he climbed out of the car. "Hey," he said, attempting to play it cool.

"Hey," Leif replied, walking over to greet him. He shoved his hands in his back pockets as though nervous. "I thought we could take my truck to the junkyard. The road in's not too forgiving. We can come back and pick your car up after."

"Yeah, sure. Okay." Not that Russ cared, but he was happy to go along with whatever.

Leif picked up a backpack from near his truck and put it into Russ's car. "I wasn't sure if date night included a sleep-over, so I'll just throw that in, in case."

Russ couldn't have stopped his grin if he'd tried. "I'm not opposed to sleepovers."

Leif laughed and they climbed into his truck. It was an old Dodge, dented and rusted, and the inside smelled like a mix of motor oil and dirt.

"She's old, but she's never let me down yet," Leif said as he started her up. She rumbled to life.

Russ grinned. "My pop had one just like it. Smells just the same."

Leif's smile was warm, and he threw her into gear and they bumbled down the road. The junkyard was only a ten-minute drive, but yeah, the road in was more potholes than road. The junkyard itself was a fenced compound, with the rusted carcasses of cars and trucks in piled rows. There was a small shop at the front, also rusted and dented, but Leif took a big black plastic storage tub from the back of his truck and walked in like he owned the place.

An older man, pudgy and smiling, wearing coveralls and a long unruly beard, came out to greet him with a warm handshake. "Been a while," he said to Leif.

"Too long, Jimmy," Leif replied. "Brought a friend with me today. Was hoping we could take a look around."

"Course, course," Jimmy said, not really even looking at Russ. "Newer stuff's in the end row. There's a stack of scrap iron that I thought you might like. Help yourself."

"You're a champion, Jimmy," Leif said, and he waved him off, nodding for Russ to follow him.

They walked past rows of cars and trucks, scraps of

rust and busted parts. It was kind of fascinating and sad that these vehicles were once loved, once a prized possession, but long forgotten now. It felt like a graveyard almost. Or an autopsy room for mechanical things. "It's kind of sad that we throw things away when we think they're no longer useful to us," Russ mused as they walked.

"It is. That's why I love reusing stuff. Giving things purpose and making them new again." Leif stopped walking and turned to face him. "I really like that you appreciate that."

That tiny little admission, that little token of recognition, made Russ's heart do stupid things. He wanted to kiss Leif so bad, but given they were in public—albeit in an obscure place and completely alone—he didn't want to ruin the mood or the glorious feeling in his chest. He simply smiled and tucked his emotions away for now.

"Oh, look at this," Leif said, finding some misshapen length of iron. "And this . . ."

And after twenty minutes, he had a small pile of odds and ends in his black tub in the middle of the dirt path. He was in his element, that was for sure. He spoke excitedly about each find and the importance of each rusty, banged-up piece of junk and how this was his favorite medium of art.

Russ could listen to him talk all day.

"You're kinda quiet," Leif said, holding what looked like an old car door handle. "Am I boring you? Does this really suck for you?"

"God no, I love it," Russ replied. "Watching you do your thing is fascinating, and I love how you see something, like that—" He nodded to the old door handle. "—and most people would think it was trash, but you see something else entirely. Like purpose and possibility. I think that's beautiful."

Leif stared at him for a beat too long, something flashing in his eyes before he looked away and laughed. "Fuck, I want to kiss you so bad," he mumbled. "You have no idea."

"I think I do," Russ whispered. "I want to kiss you too, but I didn't know if you did the in-public thing."

Leif froze, as though he needed Russ's words to make sense in his head first before he tossed the handle into the tub with the other parts. Then he took two huge steps, took Russ's face in his hands and kissed him.

It was hard and deep, frantic and passionate. It was so full of fire Russ's eyes rolled back in his head and he melted into Leif's fierce hold.

God, this man could kiss.

And when Leif broke the kiss, their breathy laughs were plumes of frost. "I think we got a little hot," he said, making Russ laugh.

He was breathless and floaty, and every cell in his body was buzzing with warmth and a pleasant hum of desire.

"You ready to go?" Leif asked when it seemed all Russ could do was smile. Leif laughed and took hold of Russ's chin. "You awake in there?"

Russ laughed off his embarrassment. "Did you find everything you were after?"

Leif looked right into his eyes and kissed him softly. "I think so, yeah."

Was he talking about the junk parts? Or something else? Russ was pretty sure he was talking about something else.

Don't get ahead of yourself. God, if wishes were horses . . .

Leif bent down to carry one side of the black tub.

"Okay, so we'll dump this back at my workshop, and you can show me your loft."

Russ grabbed the other side and helped him carry it out to his truck. *Right. The loft.* As much as Russ just wanted to take Leif back to his place and finish what that kiss had started, he did promise to show him the loft.

Russ waited at the truck while Leif paid for his stash and had a quick chat with Jimmy. And when he was done and walking back toward him with his long, confident strides and sexy-as-hell smile, Russ's heart did that weird and stupid thing again. "You ready?" Leif asked.

Was he ready? Russ was so woefully unprepared yet so long overdue for this it wasn't even funny. "Hell yes," he replied. So fucking ready.

They drove Leif's truck back to his house and Leif hefted the tub into his workshop while Russ waited outside. There didn't seem to be anyone home, or anyone in the whole street for that matter. There was nothing but vacant fields across the road and an old farmhouse way back off the road. But there was no tractor in the fields, no horses or sheep. All the neighbors were quiet or at work or the houses stood empty. Russ wasn't sure which. "Mom's at work," Leif said, as if he could read where Russ's mind had gone. "Cliff works the night shift. He's my younger brother. And Faith's at nursing school. Lindzie works at the mall. Ty and Harley both live in town now."

"Your brothers and sisters?"

Leif nodded happily. "Yep." Russ eyed the small house, wondering how on earth they had all lived in it. "They drove me crazy growing up, but I missed 'em when they moved out."

Russ understood all too well what it was like to miss your family. He was quiet on the drive back into the city.

He hadn't expected the thoughts of family to play on his mind, and he tried to rise above it, though he was pretty sure Leif could see through him.

"You know as much as I love my old truck, your car is a whole lot nicer," Leif said. "And I wouldn't like to put all my dirty gear in it though."

Russ smiled. "So that stuff you just collected from Jimmy, is that for a project at college? Or just for you?"

"Actually, it's for you."

Russ shot him a look. "For me?"

"Yeah. I'm gonna make you a better set of antlers."

"From what we collected today? There wasn't one antler-looking thing in there."

Leif laughed at that. "Because you can't see the potential in what we collected."

"Well, I could. I thought it was all great. But antlers?"

He chuckled. "Trust me. There's antlers just waiting to come to life in that tub. Not the wearable kind. More of the statue kind. Better than the ones I made for the masquerade."

"Hey, don't knock them. I happen to love those antlers." Russ wasn't even embarrassed to admit that. "They still sit on my dresser in my room."

Leif's smile was slow and salacious. "Want to wear them tonight? Or do you want me to wear them?"

Russ squirmed in his seat. He couldn't decide which he wanted more. "Undecided."

"Or we can take turns."

He pulled the car up at the curb. "Jesus. I won't even last until we get back to my place if you keep talking about it."

Leif laughed but looked out the windshield. "Why'd we

stop here? Did it become uncomfortable to drive?" He looked pointedly at Russ's crotch. "I've never had any kind of sex in a car before, but I'm not sure just how tinted these windows are."

Russ laughed. "Uh, no. As good as I'm sure that would be." He looked up at the building he was parked in front of. "This is it. The loft."

"Oh!" Leif barked out a laugh. "Well, I'm glad that's not embarrassing at all. I mean, the offer could still stand, if you want. But we are starting to lose daylight, and if you want me to see the space in natural light . . ."

Yes. Right. The loft. Get back on track, Russ. "This way." He got out and led Leif through the locked doors and through a dark vestibule to the service elevator at the end. He lifted the grill and they stepped in, closing the grill behind them. "This used to be a warehouse," Russ said, stating the obvious. He pressed the button and the old elevator clanked into use. "It was a wool press originally. I'm not sure what I'll do with the ground-level space. I'm exploring a few options, and it depends on what I do with that and next door before I ultimately decide what I want to do up here."

Russ pulled the elevator grill up and stepped out. There was still enough light; the huge windows that graced both long sides of the warehouse let in ample light, but Russ hit the switches as well.

Industrial bulbs hung from the vaulted ceiling. Huge wooden beams cast steeple-fingered shadows upward. The floor was a mishmash hopscotch of old wood and polished concrete.

"Oh my God," Leif whispered as he walked slowly out into the huge open-plan room. He looked around, his eyes huge, his mouth smiling. He turned to Russ like he'd just found the Holy Grail. "This is amazing. Don't change a thing."

Russ laughed and the sound echoed off the walls.

"The photos don't do it justice." Leif was studying the oversized brick window frame. "At all." Then he was touching everything. The walls, the pillars, the floorboards, the concrete.

"There's plumbing down this wall," Russ pointed to the far end. "So wet areas would make sense. Kitchen, bathroom. I've spoken to my builders and it's definitely possible."

Leif was walking around like he'd just stepped into a dream. "I can see why you love it. It's beautiful. Everything. The size, the proportion, the history. You have to respect the history, Russ. I wouldn't change a thing. One partition privacy wall for your bathroom and leave the rest of it open. All separate space can be allocated by soft furnishings and clever design. Exposed industrial fittings with soft lighting and plush fabrics. God." He shook his head in disbelief. "I could go so overboard in a place like this. Bold, industrialized-statement pieces that complement the design elements, and incorporate the old wool press elements. I bet I could find old lever handles from wool presses, and the wood . . . do you know what lanolin does to wood? Oh, Russ, this could be amazing."

He breathed in deep and let it out with a smile. "I know."

"But?"

"But I don't know if I want to live in it." He touched the wooden pillar next to him. "I love my house, but it's so big and there's just me. Some days I feel swamped in there, by the size of it. Some days I feel like its only purpose is to remind me that I'm alone." God, he couldn't believe he was admitting to this. "And by moving to somewhere smaller doesn't change the fact that I am. Christ, that just makes me sound freaking sad."

Leif went to him and took his hand. "No it doesn't. It makes you sound human." With his other hand, he cupped his jaw. "Can I ask you something? You don't have to tell me if you don't want to."

Russ looked into his eyes, scared of what his question might be.

"Why did you buy such a big house to begin with?" He frowned. "I mean, sure it's amazing and designed to perfection. I can appreciate that. But what made you—" He slid his hand down to Russ's chest. "—in here, decide to make that your home?"

Christ. If Leif was trying to learn something about him by asking such a simple question, he'd hit a bullseye. Russ took a deep breath and decided to open his heart wide for the first time in years. "To prove my worth," he replied quietly. "So my parents would find out and know that I succeeded. Because they told me I was good for nothing. They told me I was an abomination who would fail at life. That I was disgusting and a disgrace to their name."

Leif looked like he'd been punched in the gut. He put his hand to Russ's cheek. "Oh, Russ, I'm sorry."

"Me too. But those words fueled me, and succeeding at everything I did became my sole focus in life. But it catches up with you, you know?" He frowned, his heart heavy. "No matter how hard I tried to pretend it didn't bother me . . . It's a weight I carry with me. And I thought maybe moving into a smaller place wouldn't leave room for the void." He shook his head, angry with himself for dumping this all on Leif. The one guy he wanted to impress. "I'm sorry. I shouldn't have said anything."

Leif cupped his face in both hands and kissed him before pulling him into a fierce hug. "I want you to tell me," he murmured into the side of Russ's head. He held him tighter. "I want to know the real you, Russ. Not the public face, but the man who you are when no one's looking."

CHAPTER TWELVE

LEIF NOTICED that Russ was quiet when they arrived back at his house. Oh, he tried to smile and pretend, and busy himself, but Leif could tell he was out of sorts. And even a little pissed at himself. The truth was, things between them were so incredibly new. It was a little daunting for things to be so heavy from the beginning. But Leif could appreciate a few things: it was Christmas, and that was a hard time for a lot of people. Clearly it was for Russ. He was struggling.

But the most important thing for Leif was the fact Russ was open about it.

Yes, things were incredibly new. Things were so new, they barely existed at all. But if Leif was to consider the possibility of more dates, of anything remotely serious with Russ, he needed complete honesty.

And if Russ was having a tough time, he *should* be open about it. What kind of future could they have if one of them had to censor himself and the other one didn't want to deal with anything difficult?

The answer would be none.

And Leif thought maybe, just maybe, he would like to see what kind of future they could have.

He liked Russ. He didn't care about the huge house or nice car. And from what Leif could tell, Russ didn't care much for it either. His grin when they were in Leif's old truck had been honest and unbridled. A happiness that couldn't be faked or procured. And it was a happiness Leif was certain not many people got to see.

"Okay, so my favorite pizza place," Russ said, producing a takeout menu. "I wasn't sure what kind you prefer, so I thought I'd let you choose. I eat anything." He handed over the menu. "Caleb wanted to preorder everything, like six different types and sides, just to make sure you had every option."

Leif laughed. "He did?"

"Oh God, yes. He gave me a list of movie suggestions. Apparently I was unaware of what different types of movies might subconsciously tell you about me." Russ rolled his eyes. "I didn't even know that was a thing."

Leif snorted out a laugh. "There was a list?"

"In specific order. He's very thorough."

Leif couldn't help but laugh. "Sounds like it. Though seriously, I'm good with most movies. Action, comedy, documentary, whatever."

"Well, I haven't seen any movies in a long time. Probably in the last decade," Russ said. "So I'm pretty clueless about anything recent."

"I love movies from the 8os, if that helps," Leif offered.

"Same!" Russ replied. "God, Caleb would be horrified. I think he wanted me to suggest some artsy adaptation so you'd think I was clever, or something."

Leif laughed at that. "Well, I already think you're clever. Sounds like he read a bit too much into it."

"He wanted to make sure you were impressed," Russ said. He bit on his lip. "I mean, I did too. I want you to be impressed. But I guess I kinda blew that back at the loft."

"No you didn't." Leif gave him a smile. "I am impressed. I'll take honesty over a charade any day. I don't want you to pretend with me."

"You're the only guy I've met in a long time where I don't have to pretend." Russ licked his lips and frowned, though Leif's heart thumped in his chest at that admission. "I didn't mean to dump all this on you. I wanted tonight to be fun and I kind of ruined that, didn't I?"

"No, you didn't ruin anything." Leif was adamant, and despite his heart trying to break his ribs, he needed to return some honesty. "I'm interested in seeing where things between us could go. I know it's early, but I like you. The guy who you are with me is someone kind of special."

Russ swallowed hard, and he looked a little scared. "I am too. Interested, I mean. And yeah, it's early. But I'd like to see where it goes. And have dates, too. I would really like that. I've been trying to not get ahead." He blanched. "Not head. Christ. I've been trying to not get ahead of myself. God. Also being able to speak complete sentences around you would be great too." He put his hand to his forehead and laughed, all cute and flustered.

Leif planted a smiley kiss on his lips. "I'm not opposed to head. But let's do the date first. We can pick a pizza and a movie. I'm all for supreme pizza or vegetarian. And a classic 80s action flick. I'm thinking *Tango and Cash*. Or *Ghostbusters*."

Russ beamed. "Yes, yes, yes, and yes." Then he said, "Oh, I almost forgot!" He reached into a brown grocery bag and took out a small box. He hid it behind his back before Leif could see what it was. "I bought something for you. I thought about getting you flowers or something for our date because that's what dates do, right? But I thought that's too cliché, and you're anything but cliché, and I saw this . . . You'll probably think it's stupid and you don't have to keep it if you don't want. It was just something silly, but I saw it and thought of you . . ."

God, he was going to rupture something if he didn't take a breath. "I'm sure it'll be fine," Leif said, though he was suddenly nervous, dreading if Russ had spent a lot of money on him . . . because that was something he couldn't hope to reciprocate.

Russ handed the box over, clearly nervous but a little excited. He shook his head, still flustered. "Like I said, it was just something silly. You don't have to like it."

It was a small white box and inside was a Christmas ornament. Not just any kind of ornament, but a plastic bobblehead reindeer. Leif burst out laughing. "Are you kidding me? I love it!" He took it out and tapped its over-sized head and antlers. "It's perfect, thank you."

Russ's grin was pure relief. "You really like it?"

"I love it. It's ridiculously cute." Leif kissed him, soft and sweet. "And so are you."

Russ looked so happy he could just about burst. His smile, the light in his eyes, made Leif's stomach flip, and he put his hand to his belly.

"Oh, you're hungry," Russ said. "Let's get you fed."

So, they ordered two pizzas and streamed *Tango and Cash*. Leif kicked off his boots, sprawled out over the couch and got comfy. "We're just missing blankets and pillows," he mused, half-joking.

Russ dashed up the stairs and a moment later, a walking pile of bedding and pillows came back down. He tossed them onto Leif with a laugh, and they had one of the best first dates ever. They snuggled up on the couch in a nest of blankets and pillows, ate pizzas, and laughed their way through the movie.

Leif was very aware that Russ's bedding probably cost a small fortune, but Russ didn't care one bit. He acted like it was a twenty-dollar special from Target, and Leif really liked that about him. Nothing was sacred or out of bounds. This was his house, and it and everything in it was to be lived in, touched, used, sat in, lain on. He wasn't the 'oh my God, don't touch that, it cost me a lot of money' kind of guy. He was more of a 'my house is your house' kind of guy.

He was so normal. So very down to earth, and even if he had more money than Leif could dream of, he was decidedly normal.

Well, he was actually all kinds of extraordinary. Sweet, funny, kind, and smart.

But as far as social class went, they were at opposite ends of the spectrum. Yet finances aside, they were a perfect match.

Leif wondered if that would ever raise its ugly head. He assumed it would at some stage—if things got serious between them, how could it not? But for now, he would just let himself enjoy Russ's company.

Leif was lying down with Russ's head on his chest, and when the credits for the movie began to roll, Russ snuggled in a bit. "*Ghostbusters* next?"

"Or I was thinking we could make out for a while?" Leif suggested. When Russ looked up at him, Leif pulled him in for a kiss.

It was slow and gentle. Not the kind of kissing that went anywhere, just making out and enjoying the touches and warmth of it. "I like your intermissions," Russ murmured into the kiss.

They never watched the second movie. They never even made it upstairs. They made out until they were both sleepy and they fell asleep right there on the couch, wrapped around each other.

And that was exactly how they woke up too. Though there were soapy hand jobs in the shower, a lot more kissing, and a smiley, delicious breakfast.

Russ dropped Leif off at college, and Leif walked through the day like he was on a cloud. Dreamy and floaty, his head was swimming and his heart would flutter with every errant thought of Russ, his smile, his smell, his touch . . .

It was all so crazy fast, but it felt so right. He tried to tell himself to slow down, take it easy. But his heart had other ideas.

He pulled out his phone and sent off a quick text.

Would Thursday be too soon for Ghostbusters?

Russ replied ten minutes later.

I wish I could. I'll be out of town Thursday and Friday. Now I'm bummed.

A sad face came through in a separate text.

Leif was bummed too. Not enough to burst his bubble completely but it took the shine off it a little. Then Russ's little text bubble appeared.

We can Facetime and watch it together?

That made Leif smile, but it wasn't too practical.

Can't. The only TV's in the living room, unless
you're comfortable with my mom and
brother and sister watching it with us.

I wouldn't mind.

He wouldn't mind . . . Leif wanted to hug his phone.
Now, surely he could wait a few days to see him again . . .

How about we save it for the weekend. Will you
be back by Saturday?

Absolutely. I can be at your place early if you
want?

How early's early?

Breakfast?

LOL See you then.

LEIF DISTRACTED himself the only way he knew how—
with art. When he wasn't in class or helping his mom with
dinner or laundry, he was in his workshop. And what better
way to distract himself from thinking about Russ than to
make something for him?

All those parts he'd collected from Jimmy's junkyard
were beginning to take shape. He belted out metal, heated
it, reshaped it, welded it. He grinded it, joined it, cut it, and
he was happy with how it was coming along.

On Thursday, Jamie appeared in the doorway. "Hey,

stranger," he said. He was still chewing something, so Leif assumed he'd been in to see his mom first.

"Hey," Leif said. He put the angle grinder down and took off his goggles. "What's going on?"

"Just freezing my ass off to come check up on you," he replied. "That your millionaire boyfriend hasn't swept you off to somewhere super expensive without me."

Leif laughed. "He's not my boyfriend."

"Yet," he replied quickly, then studied Leif for a moment. "But you want him to be."

Leif tried to object, but he didn't have it in him. He was still smiling. "I . . . It's too early for that."

"Jesus, Leif."

"I know."

"You look like one of those Japanese anime porn videos where he gets all flush in the cheeks with hearts in his eyes."

"I do not."

"You do too. It's so cute it's gross."

Leif laughed. "I like him, J."

"I can see that." He touched the long, twisted metal rod Leif had been working on. "Just tell me he treats you okay."

"He does."

"He doesn't think he can just treat you like shit and fix it with all his money and gifts and stuff like that, does he?"

"J, he's not like that at all." Leif took a deep breath and let it out slowly. "Thank you for caring enough to ask and thank you for coming to check up on me. But he's not like that. I don't really know how to explain it. He has a very weird relationship with his money. It's like he resents it."

Jamie arched one eyebrow. "Yeah, right."

"I know, it sounds cliché. But he's . . . different. I dunno, J. He has everything money can buy, but the things he wants the most aren't for sale." Leif sighed. "I probably shouldn't be talking about him behind his back. It feels wrong."

Jamie nodded slowly and gave a nod to the metal cluster starting to take form. "Are these . . . ?"

"Antlers? For Russ? Yes. I thought I might give them to him for Christmas. As a gift. I mean, he knows I'm making them, so it's not really a surprise, but I can't really afford anything else. Nothing he'd like anyway. Not that he'll expect that after what he bought for me, but I don't know. I'm overthinking it."

"What he bought for you?" Jamie asked, curious and wary. "I thought you said he wasn't the kind to throw money around to impress?"

Leif smiled and leaned over so he could bop the bobble-head reindeer. "He spent all of four bucks."

Jamie's eyes went wide, as did his smile. "He bought you that?"

"Yep. As our first date gift. He said flowers were too cliché."

"Another reindeer . . . The mask, the new sculpture, and now this? Are you sure he doesn't have a fetish?"

Leif laughed. "Positive. It's really cute, don't ya think?"

Jamie flicked the bobblehead's antlers and gave Leif a smiling shake of his head. "Yeah, it's cute. Goddammit, Leif."

"What?"

He sighed dramatically. "I think I need to meet him. Officially. Like official introductions, best friend to boyfriend."

"He's not my boyfriend."

Jamie flicked the little reindeer's antlers again. "I'm sorry to be the one to break it to you, but cute bobblehead reindeer Christmas ornament gifts fall squarely in the boyfriend category." He shrugged. "That's just how it is. I don't make the rules."

Leif laughed, and as much as he tried, he couldn't have stopped smiling even if he'd wanted to. "We'll see. I'm trying not to get my hopes up, and you're not helping."

"When are you seeing him next?"

"Saturday morning." Leif's belly tightened at the mere thought.

Jamie shook his head and rolled his eyes. "Christ. You're so far gone already. He better feel the same about you. That's all I'm sayin'."

Leif laughed it off and steered the conversation off the subject of anything Russ related. He really needed to slow it down. He was getting way ahead of himself, and now he was stuck wondering if Russ did feel the same.

He'd said he was interested, and he'd said he liked him and liked spending time with him. So that was good, right?

Maybe this weekend would tell. Maybe the fantasy bubble would burst, soaking them both with a fresh dose of reality. Maybe Leif would see a different side of Russ. A side he didn't much care for . . . Maybe he had an ugly racist side, not that he seemed the type. Or maybe he was a jerk to waiters and servers in restaurants. Maybe he should conduct a few little tests on Saturday . . .

Stop overthinking it.

Just wait to see how he reacts when he sees you on Saturday morning . . .

LEIF PRETENDED he wasn't watching the clock or anything, but he was up early, showered, dressed, and scrolling through social media from the sofa that gave the best view of cars coming down the street. Not that they'd agreed on a specific time, but breakfast was anywhere from six to ten or thereabouts, and Leif was trying not to get too excited, but right at eight o'clock, Russ's car pulled into the drive.

Leif's heart was hammering, his belly full of butterflies. "Okay, Mom. Not sure when I'll be back. I'll text you though."

"Okay, love," his mom said, coming out from the kitchen. "Look at your face."

Leif stopped and scrubbed a hand over his chin. "Have I got toothpaste . . ."

"No. You look happy," she said, her eyes gleaming. "Be safe, won't you love."

"Oh God," Leif mumbled as he got out the door, grateful Russ hadn't heard that. "See you later."

Russ was getting out of his car just as Leif stepped off the front porch, and his thought came back to him.

Just wait to see how he reacts when he sees you on Saturday morning . . .

If Russ's smile was anything to go by, then yeah, maybe he felt the same. It was a grin, happy but almost relieved, but above all of that, it was genuine. The kind of happiness that couldn't be faked.

Leif was sure their smiles were a matching set.

"Morning," Leif said as he walked toward him.

"Morning," Russ replied. "Not too early I hope?"

Leif met him with a smiley kiss. "Perfect timing."

"Good," he said with a chuckle. "I considered coming at six."

He wanted to see me as much as I wanted to see him. Leif got into the car, his grin wide, his heart happy. "Where to first?"

"Well, I did promise you breakfast," he said, starting the car.

"Breakfast sounds good."

"Then I thought I'd see what you wanted to do for the rest of the day. I wasn't sure how much time we had. If you had plans for tonight, or what time I needed to have you home."

"I do have plans for tonight," Leif said.

"Oh." Russ frowned. "I mean, that's fine. We didn't really specify."

Leif grinned at him. "My plans for tonight include you, your bed, and maybe the collar and leash I left at your place. And not much else."

Russ squirmed in his seat and cleared his throat. "We could always skip breakfast."

Leif laughed despite his hardening dick. He loved the fact Russ was turned on, and suddenly he was hungry for more than just breakfast. He took Russ's hand and pressed his palm against his erection. "We can always go out for lunch, right?"

Russ swallowed hard and hissed out a low breath. "Yeah, breakfast is overrated."

THEY BARELY MADE it up the stairs. They were a mess of frantic kissing and desperate hands, pushing and pulling until they were both naked on the bed. Leif was on his back, legs open, and Russ lay over him with both cocks in his hand. Sliding, frotting, kissing, and grinding until they both came.

They collapsed in a sweaty, chuckling, sticky mess. "We forgot the collar and leash," Russ mumbled.

"That's for round two."

Russ covered his jaw and neck with kisses and scrapes of his teeth. "Yes, please. I've been thinking about you all week," he whispered between kisses and bites. "About having you inside me, all week."

Heat bloomed in Leif's belly; his spent cock gave a twitch. He pulled Russ's face up in his hands and kissed him hard and deep.

And much later, when Leif was buried inside him, they made love. They held on tight, kissed deep and rocked slow, and Leif knew Russ felt the same. It was in his eyes. It was in the way he gasped with every thrust, how he whispered Leif's name. How he looked at him, with such honesty and soul, Leif had no doubt.

There was something starting to bloom between them. Something special. Something that could so easily become love.

Leif wanted it, and he was certain Russ wanted it too. As crazy as it seemed, it was right. His heart knew with every beat, like his body knew with every thrust, every kiss, every touch.

He was falling in love.

"WE SHOULD GO OUT," Russ murmured. They were showered and dressed, snuggled up in the couch. Some Hallmark Christmas movie was on TV and neither one of them wanted to move to find the remote control to change the channel.

"We probably should," Leif agreed.

But still, they didn't move.

"This movie is terrible."

Leif laughed. "Yeah, it kind of is." Leif had noticed this weekend something he'd missed the times he'd been here before. Russ didn't have a Christmas tree up in his house. He didn't even have one decoration. And that reminded Leif that Russ had no family and no one to celebrate Christmas with. Or Thanksgiving or birthdays or anything. He hated the idea of him being so alone at any time, but especially over the holidays. Instead of asking hard questions and souring the mood between them, he decided to keep things light. He peeled himself away and jumped up, holding his hand out. "Come on, gorgeous. Let's go find something for dinner."

Which was a great idea until every restaurant and storefront had Christmas decorations. Lights, trees, candles, music. If Leif was trying to shield Russ from the festivity, then going out for dinner the week before Christmas was the worst idea.

But Russ suggested a small Italian restaurant and he promised they had the best pasta in town, so Leif didn't object. They hung their coats over the backs of their chairs, unwound their scarves, and sat opposite each other at a small private table.

"I feel like I should apologize," Leif said. "Suggesting dinner when everything's so Christmassy. I know you're not a fan."

"I'm not, no. But I have to eat. And you look really cute in this lighting."

Leif chuckled, relieved. He leaned in and whispered, "Pretty sure it's the sex glow."

Russ barked out a laugh. "Is that a thing?"

"Oh yeah. And we have it."

He sipped his water, his cheeks a rosy red. "Maybe tomorrow we could do something else. Go for a drive. Go to the museum or the art gallery. Or go-kart racing. Or horse riding."

"That all sounds great. But . . ." He paused for effect. "And I'm not keeping tabs or anything, but we still haven't used the collar and leash again, and it's your turn to top me. Unless you're up for round three when we get back to your place tonight."

Russ looked around to see if anyone heard, but no one had. He leaned in and motioned for Leif to do the same. "You shouldn't talk like that. I haven't had this many hard-ons since high school. It makes sitting in restaurants awkward. Or just being in public in general."

Leif laughed. "Round three tonight then."

They were interrupted by their server, and Leif had to cover his laugh when Russ shifted in his seat. But they managed to order, and they managed to eat too, around small talk and flirty smiles.

"So, I've been thinking," Russ said casually. "That I'd like to see a showcase of your work. Does your college have an exhibition or a showroom?"

Leif took his time swallowing his food, giving himself a few seconds to get his thoughts in order. "Uh, sure. Can I ask why?"

"I'm interested in you," he replied, and his cheeks grew pink in the muted light. "I'm interested in what you do and what you want to do when you finish school. Do you want a career in art?"

"Sure. I'd love it, but it doesn't exactly pay the bills. I'll always make art, even if I have to wait tables or stock shelves to get by. Art is my life. It's not what I do, it's who I am."

"I've only seen photos, not counting the antler head-wear, which is awesome."

"I made them out of twigs."

He smiled at that. "Just proves how good you are."

Leif really didn't think they were centerpiece worthy, but he didn't say that. "They do have some of our work on display," Leif added. "At college. But they're closed now until after Christmas. I have some at home in my workshop. But I'm working on your real antler piece, so you might have to wait. I wanted it to be a surprise."

"You're really making something just for me?"

Leif nodded. "Yeah. It's going to be your Christmas present." Russ looked ready to object, so Leif put his hand up. "I want to make this for you, and you've already given me something, so it just makes us even."

"What have I given you?"

"My little bobblehead reindeer."

"That hardly counts. It was a few dollars on a display at the checkout line."

"The cost doesn't matter. You said you saw it and thought of me. You said it made you smile, and that's all I need."

Russ met his gaze and it seemed to take him a second to blink or breathe, and in the end a smile won out. "You're kind of great, you know that?"

Now it was Leif who blushed. "Just kind of?"

"Shut up, you know what I mean." He took another drink of water, and his brow pinched as though he was trying to decide how to say what else he had to say. "I uh, I'm not too good at telling people what I think of them or how they make me feel. I haven't had much luck with relationships, of any kind, to be honest. Family, friends, lovers . . ."

Leif's heart squeezed for him. "I think you're doing just fine. And everyone's different. There is no wrong or right, no timelines, no rules. We can make our own."

Russ laughed quietly and shook his head. When he met Leif's gaze, his eyes were penetrating. "How do you always know what to say?"

"Because I'm kind of great, remember?" Leif turned his water glass a quarter turn and looked back into his eyes. "And for what it's worth, Russ, I think you're kind of great too."

He blushed, but his smile was all kinds of fantastic. "Have you had enough to eat?"

"I have, thank you."

"Are you ready to leave? Or would you like to take a stroll through town? The Christmas lights are pretty. Or we could grab a drink at Evoque? It's not far from here."

Leif weighed up his options. "They all sound great, and maybe we can have a drink and hit the dance floor another night. But I think I'd like to go back to your place. We still need to watch *Ghostbusters*."

"We do."

"And the truth is," Leif admitted, "I'm not ready to share you just yet."

Russ's face lit up; his smile was brilliant if a little shy. But he paid the bill and Leif noticed a few of the other customers looking their way. Clearly they recognized Russ and were probably wondering who the hell Leif was, but Russ was oblivious. He simply put his hand to the small of Leif's back as they walked out the door and held his hand as they walked to the car.

When they got in the car, Russ started the engine, but he didn't put the car into gear. Instead, he turned in his seat, his smile truly beautiful. "I'm really glad I met you. I wasn't going to go to the masquerade ball. I really wasn't. But Caleb insisted and I thought it was going to be the same old guys, the same conversations . . ." He sighed, still smiling. "But you walked in."

Leif's heart thudded at his words and at how intimate it was in the car. A confined, quiet space. "I did. And there was this *Assassin's Creed* guy who was sexy as hell."

Russ laughed. "And you didn't recognize me."

"I had no clue. Which is kind of embarrassing, really."

Russ reached over and took his hand. "It was the best part, if I'm being honest."

"I'd really like to get to know you," Leif said quietly. "The real you."

Russ's eyes flinched, and he studied the dashboard for a few seconds. His fingers stilled on Leif's hand. "You know me better than most people. Guys are usually just interested in the name or publicity, ya know? No one's ever really interested in me."

Leif threaded their fingers. "I am. The real you."

Russ's gaze met his and they simply stared into each other's eyes. The inside of the car suddenly felt far too small, the air impossibly static. But Russ managed a small laugh and kissed the back of Leif's hand. "We should go."

Leif kept his hand on Russ's thigh as he drove. There was no need for words. They'd just made some bold and wonderful declarations, and that was all they needed for now. Leif wanted to bask in that for as long as it lasted.

Coming into Russ's house through the garage, they found themselves in the kitchen. Russ instructed the lights to come on, and the house lit up to a warm glow. The soft lighting eliminated any sharp edges and drew the vast spaces in close, and Leif was about to comment on how much he loved his house when he saw blueprints on the kitchen counter. "What are those?"

"The loft," Russ replied. He let out a sigh, and a perplexed line marred his brow.

"You're so undecided."

He nodded.

"Isn't that answer enough?" Leif asked.

"What do you mean?"

"If you're so unsure, then something in your mind is trying to tell you something." Leif stepped in close and put his hand to Russ's chest. "Or maybe it's your heart."

"My heart . . . ?"

Leif cupped Russ's face and pressed him against the kitchen counter. He didn't want him to turn or walk away from him. "Perhaps this house isn't the problem," Leif said gently. "And the loft isn't a solution."

Russ kept his gaze down, his voice quiet. "What do you mean?"

"Moving into a smaller place won't fix anything. How can it when the void you're trying to replace is inside you? What's missing is your family and the gaping hole they created. They removed your choice and left you with the consequences, and that's a really shitty thing to do. I'm not saying you *should* forgive them."

"I couldn't handle their rejection again," he admitted quietly. "I just couldn't. And what if they decide only to tolerate me because of the money? I couldn't . . . I can't . . ." He shook his head and sighed. "I built this empire, this portfolio to prove to them I was better than they thought. Spite is a powerful thing. Succeeding just to piss them off was what drove me for a lot of years. But in the end, maybe it's because of that I don't want to reach out. I don't even know if I could forgive them. What kind of parents disown their own kid? I don't know if I want that kind of person in my life."

"Russ, they created a hole in your life. They took that power from you, and you've been trying to fill that hole. It's not the void you need to fix. But you need to take back the power."

"You think I should contact them?"

"If you want to, then yes."

"But? It sounds like there's a but coming."

"But," Leif said gently. "I was thinking more of letting them go."

Russ's face crumpled and his chin wobbled, but he didn't cry. "I know."

"It won't be easy," Leif offered. "But I'll be around. If you want me to be."

Russ scoffed out a laugh. "I would like you around, very much."

"It's not a decision you need to make right now. And you can always do both. Formulate a plan and take control; you can extend an olive branch to them. If they're open to accepting you as you are, then great. If they're not, then you can decide to end it. It'll be on your terms, and yes, it'll suck and be horrible, but then you can begin to heal."

"You seem to know a lot about it."

"I had to say goodbye to my family. Not literally, but in my heart I did. I went into foster care when I was real little, and there was always the hope your parents would come back. But mine didn't. And then I realized that my new family, the ones who took me in and loved me, *were* my real family. I remember thinking on my thirteenth birthday that my birth parents might come and surprise me, and of course they didn't. And that night for dinner, Mom cooked my favorite meatloaf and we had birthday cake and everyone sang "Happy Birthday" and I remember looking around at my family, with all my foster brothers and sisters, and realized what I thought I'd been missing, I had all along. My life got a whole lot better after that. I stopped wishing and started appreciating."

Russ sighed. "I don't have a foster family," he mumbled. "I don't have . . . that."

"Then make one. Begin a group for other displaced and abandoned queer folk and find some new brothers and sisters. Did you know that elderly queer people in nursing homes are less likely to have any visitors, ever. Go and meet some, take pudding and Jell-O, or sneak in some bourbon and play cards once a week, or start an art class with them. They can be your new grandparents." Leif smiled. "Family is what you make it, Russ."

"You make it sound easy."

"It's not. And it won't be. But it *will* be worth it." Leif kissed his cheek, his closed eyelid.

"This year feels different," Russ admitted in a whisper. "This year has been harder than I remember. For eleven months of the year, I barely think of them at all. Then December comes along and it begins . . . It used to be a niggling thought, but now it feels like a—" He put the heel of his hand to his chest. "—like a sucking chest wound, like I've been ripped open. I can't . . . makes breathing hard, I don't know . . ." He sighed with a frown. "I don't want to be alone this Christmas. Not even that I don't *want* to be alone, I don't think I *should* be alone this Christmas. I don't know what this is. Or why this year in particular. But it's just harder this year than it has been all the other years."

Leif's heart was breaking for him, and he knew what he could do to fix it. "I want you to come to my place for Christmas lunch with my family."

Russ blinked back his surprise. "Uh . . . pardon?"

"I want you to spend Christmas with me and my family.

The idea of you being alone on Christmas Day just kills me."

He frowned and struggled to answer for a long moment. "I uh . . . I normally spend Christmas evening at the soup kitchen. I do that every year on Christmas day. It keeps me busy."

"Then I'll help you. Lunch with me and my fam, then together you and I can volunteer at the soup kitchen for dinner. It'll give us a good excuse to bail early on my brothers before the too-annoying questions start. Don't get me wrong, they'll make a sport out of embarrassing me. There's always enough food, and Mom cooks the best Christmas lunches. There'll be a whole spread. Turkey with Mom's secret stuffing, bean casserole, mac and cheese, pecan pie. And my mom's Christmas cookies are the best."

Russ's whole face softened; his eyes were a little teary, and he frowned. "You'd do that with me? Lunch, then the soup kitchen?"

"Of course I would," Leif whispered, then put his forehead to Russ's. "Say yes. Say you'll spend Christmas with me."

Russ closed his eyes, but ever so slightly, he nodded. "Okay. I'd like that. Thank you."

Leif pulled him in for a crushing hug, and he held him until he felt the resistance give out, and Russ allowed himself to be held.

CHAPTER THIRTEEN

REINDEER GAMES.

That's what Leif had called the masquerade ball at Evoque. A gathering or group to which you didn't belong.

That's exactly how Russ felt as he drove to Leif's mom's house.

Not that he didn't belong with Leif. Because he was quite certain he did. But he was about to go to a family lunch, with his . . . boyfriend?

Not that they'd discussed labels either. But in Russ's head, that's what they were—boyfriends.

But no, he was about to join *a family* for Christmas. It wasn't his family. But a family nonetheless. And Leif's words came back to him. Family is what you make it. Russ knew Leif was right. He had to take back that control, the decision that was made for him, and he had to move forward. He'd been so focused on his business and his brand that he'd forgotten to take care of himself. He'd tried to outrun it, but it was time. The gaping hole his family had left in his life needed to be healed.

That healing started today.

For the first time in years, he wouldn't be alone on Christmas Day.

The sun was trying to come out from behind the clouds and the air was crisp. On the drive over, he saw kids on new bikes, new skateboards, playing with remote control cars. The cold weather did little to dampen their joy, and Russ tried to absorb some of that to quell the nerves that writhed and hissed in his belly. It was supposed to be a happy occasion, not one filled with dread.

As if it wasn't daunting enough that he was meeting Leif's entire family, but on Christmas Day?

No pressure.

Leif had given strict instructions too. He wasn't to bring a thing. No food, no flowers, no gifts. Just himself.

And Russ quite liked that about Leif. There were no expectations. He truly wanted Russ just to be himself, nothing else. Not the rich businessman, not the entrepreneur, not the name.

Just himself.

His true self.

He pulled into Leif's driveway. There were some other older cars alongside Leif's old truck. The house looked quiet from the outside, though everything appeared monochrome. The siding was grayed with age, the sky above was overcast and winter had browned off the grass, the trees were bare.

Leif walked out onto the porch, smile wide, and just like that, Russ's day got a whole lot brighter. He was wearing his black jeans, a red lumberjack flannel shirt, his blond hair was swept up, and Russ's heart banged hard inside his chest. He climbed out of his car just as Leif stepped onto the grass and he greeted him with a kiss. "Merry Christmas, handsome," Leif said. He took Russ's hand and led him toward the house. "You ready for this?"

"I think so," Russ whispered. Christ, he could commandeer a boardroom with big-name execs, but he felt so out of his league. "Reindeer games, huh?"

Leif stopped at the bottom of the steps and faced him. "What?"

"Nothing, I just . . . You said that to me the night we met, and . . . Never mind."

"You're not an outsider here," Leif said. He put his hand to Russ's jaw and thumbed his cheek. "You belong here. You'll see."

And with a squeeze of his hand, Leif led him up the porch steps and through the front door. And if the outside was monochrome and cold, the inside was color and warmth. The living room was small, cozy, filled with people, and it was loud. Six people filled every available space—on the couch, in a chair, sprawled on the floor in front of the fire. They were talking and laughing with each other; one guy tossed a sofa cushion to the girl in front of the fire.

"Guys," Leif said. "This is Russ. Russ, this is Faith, Cliff, Lindzie, Ty, and that's Harley. These are my brothers and sisters."

"Hey," Cliff said first. Then the others followed with some form of hello.

Russ gave a wave. "Uh, hi."

Then a voice called out from the kitchen. "Table, please."

And like clockwork, everyone got up, some shoved and pushed, but they all smiled and they began to set the table. A potted plant was taken off the dining table, replaced with plates, cutlery, jugs of water, cups, salt and pepper, and baskets of bread and butter. Chairs were arranged and straightened, and it reminded Russ a little of those pitstop crews in car races. Fast, efficient, no fuss.

They must have done this hundreds of times.

Maybe every dinner, of every day, for years.

It made Russ smile.

Then a woman came out into the living room, wiping her hands on a dishtowel. She was thin, maybe five foot four, with short, graying hair, bright eyes and a wide, warm smile. "Oh, my goodness," she said, coming toward them. "You must be Russ. Leif told me you'd be coming. Merry Christmas, and thank you for putting a smile on my boy's face."

Russ almost died, but Leif laughed and gave him a squeeze. "Thank you for having me."

"More the merrier," she said. "Now boys, help put the dishes on the table."

Was it weird to be given chores as a guest in a house? Russ didn't think so. In fact, it made him feel part of the bigger picture. Helping Leif as they took casserole dishes and trays from the oven to the table, to a room full of talking and laughing people, felt kind of nice. They sat down next to each other at the large, crowded table to a lunch of amazing food. There was turkey, baked potatoes, different casseroles, and mac and cheese. Homecooked, made with love, for love.

It was the best meal Russ could remember eating in a long time.

They all spoke of a time and of people Russ didn't know, but he never once felt excluded. It was funny and familial, and he found himself laughing along. Leif had his hand on Russ's thigh as he told a story from their childhoods. No one cared who Russ was, no one asked him questions or put him under the interrogation lights.

Maybe Leif had told everyone not to pry and to leave him alone, but regardless, he felt very welcome.

And Leif's mom sat at the head of the table, smiling at her brood as they all jibed and laughed. Her gaze caught Russ's and her smile became something else. A mom's smile, one that *knew*, one that understood. One he hadn't seen in far too long and one he missed with a sudden ferocity.

A lump of emotion formed in Russ's throat, and he gave her a nod. Her face softened and she nodded back and before anyone could notice the silent exchange between them, she said, "Okay, who wants coffee and cookies?"

Leif, Ty, and Lindzie stood up. "I'll get it."

"No, I'll get it," they argued and all bustled into the kitchen.

Russ laughed with the others and Leif's mom gave him a smile and the perfect distraction. They tidied up the plates and trays and reset the table with coffee cups and a tray of gingerbread cookies.

"We do this every year," Faith told Russ, gesturing to the intricately designed and iced cookies. "It's our tradition thing."

"It's amazing," Russ replied.

Soon they were all sipping coffee and eating gingerbread, and Harley told their mom to go sit in her comfy recliner. Apparently another family tradition was that after lunch, she watched *A Miracle on 34th Street* with a fresh coffee while all the kids cleaned up the kitchen. Even as grown adults, they all still did their part. They did it bickering, and there was more shoving and pushing, but it was all in fun and their laughter made Russ smile.

The fact they were adults and still came back to spend

time with and spoil their mom told Russ all he needed to know about this family. All foster kids from all walks of life, all loved and respected exactly as they were.

"Everyone do their part," their mom called out. "Except for Leif. He's excused. He has something to show Russ in the workshop."

"I bet he does," Cliff said, waggling his eyebrows.

Leif laughed, flipped him the bird, then pulled Russ out the back door, leaving a roomful of laughter behind them. They crossed the yard to a small standalone garage, and Leif opened the huge door. "My workshop," he said, flipping on the lights. But he stopped Russ from coming in. "Close your eyes."

Russ did as he was asked, smiling. Leif led him in and closed the door behind them, shutting out the wind.

He kept his eyes closed and inhaled deeply. It smelled like a mechanic's shop or a welder's shed. Somehow it smelled familiar. "Smells like my grandpa's garage."

Leif laughed and took his hand and slowly walked him farther inside. He stopped and Leif was close enough that Russ could feel his body warmth, smell his deodorant, his scent.

"Okay, open your eyes."

Russ did, and it took him a second to realize what he was seeing.

On the workbench that ran the width of the back wall sat a sculpture. It was a reindeer head, made of rusted, bent and shaped metal, welded to form the skull, and there was a three-feet tall cascade of metal spires in the shape of antlers. There was all kinds of bits and pieces; the car door handle formed the reindeer's jaw.

It was a blackened-rusty color and intricately crafted.

That box of rusted junk they'd collected together now stood fully formed into an exquisite piece of art.

Russ's mouth was open, his eyes were wide. He turned to Leif and struggled to get words out. "You made this?"

He nodded. "For you."

Russ put his hand to his mouth, and his eyes welled with tears. "It's . . . I've never . . . Leif, it's incredible. I don't know what to say. I'm speechless."

Leif threw his arms around him and pulled him in for a hug, wrapping him up so completely. "Merry Christmas."

Russ nodded against him and allowed his emotions to surface. "Merry Christmas," he mumbled through his tears.

Leif just held him tighter and pushed him against the workbench to the side. He leaned against him, aligning their bodies perfectly, and he pulled back to cup Russ's face and kiss him. It wasn't passion and fire, but tender and adoring. When the kiss ended, Leif studied his eyes. "You okay?"

Russ nodded. "Yeah. Sorry. I wasn't expecting to be so overwhelmed."

"Don't ever apologize," Leif murmured. "But you like it?"

Russ turned his head to look at the sculpture, the side of his head fitting perfectly against Leif's throat. "I love it. It's amazing. You're amazing."

He chuckled. "Thanks."

"I mean it, Leif. You need to show your art. You need exhibits and a website. Go big and go public, because the world needs to see what you're capable of."

Leif laughed again, but Russ tilted his face so he'd look at him and see the seriousness in his eyes. "I mean it. You're incredible. The world needs to know your name."

There was a loud knock on the garage door. "Am I interrupting? Because I don't mind watching."

Leif laughed. "Jamie." He turned toward the door. "Come in."

Russ recognized the guy who let himself in as the same guy who had been dressed as the kitty cat at the masquerade. "Well, hello there," Jamie said, looking at Russ. He held his hand out to shake while Leif made introductions. "You were the sexy *Assassin's Creed* guy."

"And you were the sexy kitty with the harness and the cat-o'-nine-tails."

Jamie laughed. "That's me." He eyed the sculpture, then Leif. "It's finished! Looks great, man."

"Thanks."

He turned to Russ. "You like it?"

"I love it," Russ replied, smiling at Leif. "He's incredibly talented."

"That he is. Cute too." Jamie picked up something off the bench and held it up. Russ realized it was the bobble-head reindeer ornament he'd given to Leif. "Not as cute as this little guy though."

Leif snatched it out of his hand and put it back on the counter. "Leave it alone. I told you I loved it."

Russ wasn't sure if Jamie was joking or not, but Jamie crossed his arms and sized Russ up. "I was telling Leif before that little plastic bobblehead reindeer are strictly a boyfriend thing."

"A boyfriend thing?"

"Yeah. Like a gift that only boyfriends give each other," Jamie said. "So, is that where you're at?"

Leif groaned. "Jamie, please stop. If you're trying to do the big 'he's my best friend' speech, it's not working."

Jamie looked up at him. "I was trying to act tough."

Leif rolled his eyes. "It needs some work."

Russ smiled at their obviously close friendship, but he

was getting the 'are you good enough to be his boyfriend?' speech from the best friend. He swallowed hard. "I'm not opposed to that."

"You're not opposed to my tough-guy speech?" Jamie asked. He looked so hopeful it was hard not to smile.

"No, the boyfriend thing," Russ replied. He risked a glance at Leif. "If you're not opposed to it, that is."

Leif's grin was instant. "I'm not opposed."

Jamie clapped his hands together. "You're welcome! Right, now let's establish some ground rules." He counted off on his fingers. "One. Complete monogamy. Don't know if you've discussed that, but infidelity is a deal-breaker for Leif. Two, his art is not a hobby. It's important and it's who he is. Don't try and change that."

Russ found himself smiling. "I wouldn't. I was just telling him he needs to start doing it for a living."

"You were?" Jamie asked.

Russ nodded. "Yeah. And I'm completely on board for rules one and two."

"Good." Jamie held up his next finger. "Three. I'm the best friend. You can't get rid of me."

"Jamie," Leif said quietly. "Mom's gingerbread cookies are in the green tin on top of the fridge."

He brightened. "They are?"

Leif nodded.

"Okay then," Jamie said, walking toward the door. "You kids be good."

And with that, he slipped outside. Russ laughed and Leif shook his head. "Seriously. To get rid of him, you only have to mention my mom's baking."

"Duly noted." Russ pulled Leif against him and looked up into those blue eyes. "I meant what I said about being your boyfriend."

Leif nudged his nose to Russ's before kissing him softly. "Me too."

"I'm good with those rules too."

Leif kissed him. "Same."

"Can I be honest with you?"

He frowned. "Of course."

"I was kind of dreading today. I mean, I wanted to come here, even though I was dreading the emotions that would come with it. But it's been amazing. And your family is great. And I miss my family, and I'm sorry they want nothing to do with me, but what you said the other night was true. I need to let go and make my own family. I need to take back the power they took from me. And today was the first step in doing that. So thank you."

Leif gave him a sad smile, cupped his face with both hands, and kissed him. "You deserve to be happy and to be loved." He swallowed hard, and Russ's heart almost stopped beating. "I think I could be falling in love with you. I know it's been crazy fast, but you get me. You understand me and you like my art, and you don't care that I'm still at college."

"I think I'm falling in love with you too," Russ whispered. "I thought it was just my stupid heart trying to cling to the first good thing in my life. But it's more than that."

Leif kissed him with smiling lips. "It is. We are."

Russ took a deep breath and closed his eyes, leaning into his embrace. "We need to go to the soup kitchen . . . I wish we could stay here longer."

"We have all the time for what comes next. Later tonight, we can make love till morning, and we have next week and next year," Leif murmured against the side of his head. "I'm not going anywhere."

Russ's heart was so happy he could almost burst. "You were right about the loft too."

"I was?"

Russ nodded. "Yeah. Maybe I need to think of another use for it."

"It's a great space."

"I still want you to help design it. Maybe those art classes you talked about. Or a gallery. Or a creative center for LGBT kids who've been abandoned." Russ shrugged. "I don't know yet. But if I want to make my own family and make my life better, then I need to start with me. You've given me a lot to think about."

Leif smiled and leaned his forehead to Russ's. "You're amazing."

"Actually, I'm not really. I work a lot, I'm up early, home late. I travel a lot with my work. I get stressed, and I'm probably not easy to be around."

"And I spend far too much time in my workshop, which probably gets annoying. I'm sure we'll figure it out."

"If you spending time in here produces sculptures like this," he said, nodding to the reindeer antlers, "it's time very well spent."

"I'm so glad you like them."

"I love them. I just wish I got you something better than that silly bobblehead toy."

"Hey," Leif said, pulling back. "Don't knock my gift. I happen to love it."

"It pales in comparison to what you gave me."

Leif pinched Russ's chin between his thumb and finger and pulled him in for a kiss. "I dunno. This year for Christmas I got you, so that wins everything."

Russ laughed. "And I got you."

"You sure did. But that means you also got my five crazy siblings, a mom who will ask you—in front of other people—

if you're using protection. Oh, and there's also an over-the-top best friend."

Russ sighed happily. "Sounds perfect to me."

Leif kissed him softly. "Merry Christmas, Russ."

"Merry Christmas."

The End

ABOUT THE AUTHOR

N.R. Walker is an Australian author, who loves her genre of gay romance. She loves writing and spends far too much time doing it, but wouldn't have it any other way.

She is many things: a mother, a wife, a sister, a writer. She has pretty, pretty boys who live in her head, who don't let her sleep at night unless she gives them life with words.

She likes it when they do dirty, dirty things... but likes it even more when they fall in love.

She used to think having people in her head talking to her was weird, until one day she happened across other writers who told her it was normal.

She's been writing ever since...

ALSO BY N.R. WALKER

Titles in Audio:

Blindside

Finders Keepers

Galaxies and Oceans

Nova Praetorian

Free Reads:

Sixty Five Hours

Learning to Feel

His Grandfather's Watch (And The Story of Billy and Hale)

The Twelfth of Never (Blind Faith 3.5)

Twelve Days of Christmas (Sixty Five Hours Christmas)

Best of Both Worlds

Translated Titles:

Fiducia Cieca (Italian translation of Blind Faith)

Attraverso Questi Occhi (Italian translation of Through These Eyes)

Preso alla Sprovvista (Italian translation of Blindside)

Il giorno del Mai (Italian translation of Blind Faith 3.5)

Cuore di Terra Rossa (Italian translation of Red Dirt Heart)

Cuore di Terra Rossa 2 (Italian translation of Red Dirt Heart 2)

Cuore di Terra Rossa 3 (Italian translation of Red Dirt Heart 3)

Cuore di Terra Rossa 4 (Italian translation of Red Dirt Heart 4)

Natale di terra rossa (Red dirt Christmas)

Finders Keepers (Thai translation)

Thank you for reading

REINDEER GAMES

N.R. WALKER

CPSIA information can be obtained
at www.ICGtesting.com
Printed in the USA
BVHW031112120220
572161BV00001B/155